I0788570

THE SILENCE BETWEEN THE SONGS

SONG OF THE FALLEN SWORDS
BOOK 4

RYAN KIRK

WATERSTONE
MEDIA

 Formatted with Vellum

For the readers.
The ones who shut away the noise of the world,
Crack open a book,
And lose themselves in possibilities.

1

Elora had once told Radyn that before the cities had taken to the skies, autumn had served as an annual reminder that all that was beautiful faded and died, that nothing lasted forever. Born a child of Firestone, Radyn hadn't understood. Seasons in the sky meant little, an arbitrary distinction on calendars even the elders ignored. Singers minimized the impact of seasonal changes, striving to keep the days of roughly equal length to extend the growing season. Only now did he realize how unnatural that mode of living was.

He bit into an apple sweetened by the kiss of the season's first frost. The leaves of the maples on the distant hills were a vivid collection of oranges and reds. If the sun set just right, the entire hillside would erupt as an evening fire. He and Aria had spent many evenings on the top of the mound that was Underhill, watching the fiery display, and no matter how many times he witnessed its grandeur, it never grew old.

Elora had spoken true, though. The color on the trees had peaked as leaves raced to the ground, fleeing the bitter winter winds that would soon descend from the hills. Upcoming frosts wouldn't kiss, but kill. Winter brought death, an annual reminder that the gate waited for them all.

Heavy footsteps warned him of Aria's approach. Her belly was full with their child, and she huffed as she reached the top of the mound. "I thought I might find you here."

She cast a covetous glance at his apple. He handed it to her, and she bit into it like a hunter just returned from a long hunt. "Ooh. That's good. Thanks."

He dipped his head in acknowledgment, then turned his gaze back to the gathering he was ostensibly guarding. Dozens of tables were already built, with several more almost finished. The first plates of food emerged from Underhill's kitchens, and to the west of the tables, pigs slowly roasted over charcoal fire pits. Radyn's mouth watered whenever a strong breeze carried the scent of roasting pork up the hill.

Aria recognized his thoughtful expression. "Care to share?"

Radyn swept his arm across the scene, encompassing both the feast preparations and the distant maples. "I think the cities lost something important when we lost our connection to the soil. Every day on Firestone was the same. Down here we celebrate the end of the harvest, the end of long days of hard labor. Soon the nights will grow long and we'll rest, our focus on family and home."

He looked at her stomach, and she smiled and wrapped her arms in a loving embrace around their unborn child.

"I know what you mean. There's something deeply intuitive about all of it, isn't there? I didn't grow up with seasons any more than you did, and yet now I can't imagine life without them."

A shout from below interrupted their reflections. Kaya waved at them to come down. Aria waved back, and Kaya, satisfied her message had been delivered, skipped back to the tables.

"Have you ever seen her that happy?" Aria asked.

"No, but she deserves every bit of it. Almost every part of this feast can be traced back to her in one way or another. The boundary that keeps us safe is powered by Engine shards she grew. Much of the food came from a city that only exists because she saved it. Even the pigs are a gift from our neighbors for services she provided."

Aria shook her head and pointed. Kaya mingled with a young Singer from Firestone named Orenil. Radyn knew of him, but little else. Kaya leaned in close as Orenil bent his head to whisper something into her ear that made her giggle. "I think she's happy because of that."

"Are they together?"

Aria laughed, a sound that never ceased to warm Radyn's spirit. "For someone so observant, you have some impressive blindnesses." She tugged at his hand. "Let's go."

Radyn let his eyes drift over the horizon one last time, but nothing in the sky or on the ground threatened their gathering. Even the banti had learned to keep well away from Underhill. Though the human spirits sheltering within must have been tempting targets, those that dared come too close never lived long enough to repeat the mistake.

He wasn't the gathering's only protection. Tanwen and the other dragons, who had feasted earlier, circled overhead, and Kaya and Aria's boundary provided an extra layer of protection. The harvest festival would be as safe as anything could be on the surface. Still, Radyn found it too easy to imagine the various disasters that could befall them. He'd gotten much better at such imaginings over the course of Aria's pregnancy.

Miranda was the first to greet the couple, bowing slightly as they reached the bottom of the mound. She winked at Radyn. "I'm impressed Aria convinced you to join us."

"It's not wise to refuse the requests of a pregnant wife."

Aria elbowed him in the side. "He would have come on his own. He just needed to work up his courage to be among so many people."

"Is there anything I can do to help?" Radyn asked.

Miranda shook her head. "I know Jyn is looking for you, as is the representative from Skystone. You can't hide from them by working chores for me."

"It was worth the try."

Miranda excused herself to welcome another group of new arrivals. She greeted them warmly and was embraced by many in the group in return. Aria caught Radyn's thoughtful gaze and guessed what lay behind it. "She was right to insist on the celebration. We need this more than we thought."

There was a restrained joy in the air, evidenced by the easy smiles and laughter that rippled uncertainly through the gathering. The original soulkeepers who had founded Underhill had worked side by side with Firestone's survivors over the past several months. Radyn couldn't measure the sweat and blood spilled by all in the incredible effort to prepare for the winter, but even now, the soulkeepers gathered around certain tables, while those from Firestone collected around others.

Complicating the mix were the unexpected arrivals from Skystone and a couple of the other cities, each of which had formed into their own little impenetrable groups. Of the closest cities, only Nightkeep wasn't present, for the obvious reason that they hadn't been invited. The Engines of the surviving cities continued to deteriorate, and Underhill's tenuous success gave the clans hope a path to survival remained. All that was well and good, but the divisions that had marked them in the sky remained, even when they walked a land that didn't tolerate the weaknesses that division caused.

Radyn wandered in Kaya's direction, but Aria pulled him away with a look that told him the Singer was not to be bothered. They spoke with Nikki briefly, but the investigator was more interested in learning about the various representatives from the other cities than talking to them. They found Jyn at the end of a long journey through the crowds, drinking tea with the representative from Skystone, a handful of Singers, and Magni. Bows were exchanged, and Radyn and Aria were invited to join the table.

As they sat, the representative from Skystone bowed once again. His dark uniform carried the pins of a Sword on his shoulder, though Radyn might have guessed as much from a look. His height wouldn't impress anyone, but he carried enough muscle on his bones even Tanwen would consider him a full meal. Piercing blue eyes shone under a head shaved clean, and he carried himself with a casualness that Radyn would have called affected, as though easy smiles and a relaxed posture would convince anyone he wasn't dangerous.

The representative flashed a smile. "Senior Sword Radyn, it's an honor to meet you. I'm Senior Sword Veylan from Skystone. Legends of your strength and skill have spread far and wide."

Radyn dipped his head to accept the compliment. When he'd been younger, he would have beamed like a fool to receive such praise from a foreign senior Sword, but the praise rang hollow today. Whatever legend he possessed had come at the cost of a great number of lives, and that wasn't the legacy he wanted to pass down to his unborn daughter. "You're too kind."

Veylan poured a cup of tea and changed the subject. "I was just speaking with your Blade and complimenting him on your tremendous efforts. When we'd heard Firestone had fallen, we feared the worst."

"Thank you. A tremendous number of people have fought to prevent just that."

"Do you think what you've done here can be reproduced in other ruins?"

Veylan's gaze never shifted from Radyn's face, his intensity revealing the question was one of the true reasons he'd accepted the invitation to join their harvest festival. A loud cheer went up from a table behind them, answered by another table nearby.

"It seems possible, but I'm hesitant to call our efforts a success yet."

Veylan gestured toward the tables filled with food. "You don't call this success?"

"We have enough to survive a winter, and if we assume other summers are like this one, then yes, we have enough to continue to survive."

"But?" Veylan prompted.

"But we still don't know why similar ventures haven't succeeded. Our histories have gaps large enough for our cities to fly through, and until we solve those riddles, we're no better than explorers diving deeper into a cave with nothing but a lantern for light, never knowing what dangers lie beyond the next turn of the passage."

Veylan rubbed slowly at his clean-shaven chin as he weighed Radyn's argument. Finally he said, "A cautious answer from one whose name is whispered with awe among the strongest Blades of our generation. Yet you risk your wife and unborn child in the same environment you'd keep from city-dwellers."

The brush of Aria's shoulder against his kept his rising anger tightly restrained. He breathed slowly before answering. "I'm sure you know by now our choice to settle here was not wholly our own."

Veylan waved his hand, dismissing the comment as though shooing away a mosquito. "Come now, with your skills you could have sought refuge in any city across the continent. I mean no offense, but my point is simple. I look around and I see what you've accomplished, and I wonder why we aren't all landing at the nearest ruins."

Aria reached under the table and rested her hand on his knee, and the distraction broke through his budding anger. Veylan's questions were barbed, but they weren't meant to hook Radyn. He only wanted to reach the truth. To a sky-bound Manirah, Underhill might seem a paradise.

"I'm confident in my ability to protect my family. I'm not confident the Manirah can protect the cities if they land," Radyn said.

"There might well come a day when we no longer have the choice," Veylan observed.

"All the more reason to ensure we're learning all we can now."

Jyn raised a glass to interrupt the exchange. "I choose to mark today as an auspicious beginning to a new age. I would never have decided to make a life on the surface on my own, but I'm convinced now the soulkeepers have always had the right idea. The surface is our hope in the future. Thanks to the soulkeepers who prepared the way, and thanks to the generosity of Skystone and all our allies, we have a chance unlike any seen in generations. May our future be brighter than our past."

Those gathered around the table raised their cups and glasses, accepting the toast gladly.

Radyn took a sip only, then put his cup down.

Jyn spoke well. Today could mark a new beginning, a future in which he could finally retire Elora's maniblade and focus on shaping the world to come. The peaceful summer, filled with long days in the fields and short nights with Aria, had surprised him with a revelation. He had good friends in Jyn, Magni, Miranda, Kaya, Nikki, and so many more. He had a place for his head he looked forward to every night. Food wasn't a worry, at least for a time.

He hadn't really been searching for it, but somehow, he'd still found contentment. He took another sip of the tea, savoring the flavor of the drink. If his future held more days like this, what more could he ask for?

His good cheer lasted until the unseen attack brought every single Manirah in the area to their knees.

2

The Seer alighted from the dragon and stretched tired legs. Once, when he'd been a Singer, he'd flown often, but since accepting a new master and donning the mantle of the Seer, his travel had become almost nonexistent. It was much easier to hide his doings on paper than in person, and letters and reports found him more easily if he remained in one place. Such was the power of the written word that he'd birthed his movement as much with ink and paper as with blood and sweat.

He'd never imagined that orchestrating the downfall of humanity would be such an administrative affair.

But no, one couldn't discount the power of writing. Accurate ledgers were all that stood between a city and starvation. Ancient maps kept the cities safe from the giant nuddu that sought to devour the Engines and the humans who depended on them. And it was old and tattered histories, researched with painstaking care, that had led him here.

He breathed in deeply, filling his lungs with the thicker air of the surface. Rain had passed over these bogs the night before, and his nose caught the full-bodied scents of wet moss and the slightly sweet smell of decaying leaves. Such a combination of scents could never be found within the sterile farmlands that served as the surface of the cities, and he welcomed the smell like a long-lost old friend.

It was for the bogs and the grasslands and the mountains and those that rightfully called this world home that he fought, righting an ancient wrong.

A small crowd had gathered for his long-awaited arrival. He'd brought several of his own warriors along, and the two groups quickly formed lines that gazed warily across the space separating them. They were allies of convenience, a fact well understood by both sides, and a wrong step would be a sure way to doom this work before it truly began.

He paused a moment and allowed his eyes to wander over the environment that welcomed him. Tall pines surrounded an area that couldn't decide whether it wanted to be lake or land. The ground underfoot was soft, the Seer's boots sinking up to his toes. Behind him, the dragon lifted his feet as though disgusted with the mud caught between his massive claws.

The terrain wasn't as interesting as the people gathered to greet him. Each was tall and lean, their legs long and well-suited for walking miles in pursuit of food and shelter. They carried an assortment of weapons. The Seer spotted swords and bows easily, but several had knives hidden under their rough garments. They looked like dangerous people in a dangerous land, and that was only to the eye.

To the Seer's elevated senses, connected to the shadow song that served as his master, they were far more dangerous than they looked. Their auras swirled with powers forged through a lifetime of battling for survival in a land that didn't want them. The Seer wasn't without skill, but he would die in moments if he tried to fight the assembly before him.

So he bowed.

Those behind him were too well-trained to reveal their surprise, but he felt it in the weight of their gazes. They might serve him, but their hearts were still corrupted from exposure to the clans and their beliefs. Pride had no place here, not when their actions today would determine the fate of the world. A halting moment later, those who'd followed him on the dragon followed his lead and bowed.

When the Seer rose from his bow, it was to the vicious grins of their allies. To them, the city-born must look weak and flabby, unsuited for the gifts the Makers had bestowed upon them so many generations ago. Perhaps they watched the Seer and wondered about the taste of his flesh. In a land of such scarce resources, no source of food could be wasted. One man, shorter than most, stepped forward and spoke to the Seer in the modern language of the cities. "The way is clear."

The Seer's eyes flickered down to the man's hands, spattered with blood. "Thank you for clearing the way. They did not see reason?"

The man, named Belzrak, shrugged, the murder of an entire clan nothing more than a slight inconvenience. "There are still many who believe in the teachings of the Elders, that we deserve this. They fought hard, but they had grown soft."

Ironic, that the Seer needed to kill those who most closely understood the truth. Belzrak fought to keep his clan alive and punish the cities, not knowing the Seer's true purpose. He kept his face expressionless. "Will you lead the way?"

Belzrak nodded and turned on his heel. The line of his warriors parted to let him pass, and the Seer hurried to keep close behind him. Both Belzrak's and the Seer's warriors remained behind in an uneasy truce.

The lean warrior's trail led straight into the bog, and the Seer matched his footsteps as closely as he could. The bog would swallow him whole if he gave it the chance, the world always hungry to devour an unwary human. Belzrak walked with a confident stride. After passing a particularly wet section of trail, they came upon firmer ground littered with the bodies of the dead. His escort stepped over them, the corpses no more than annoyances. The Seer imagined his allies feasting tonight, and the thought turned his stomach.

Let them have their barbaric ways. All would be wiped clean soon enough.

He stopped to examine the bodies, struck by the realization that their deaths had not all come at the edge of a blade or the point of an arrow or spear. Lacking time to observe as closely as he would have liked, he said, "You have more ways to kill than I'd thought."

He could hear the grin in Belzrak's voice. "That we do."

The Seer pressed his lips together and returned his focus to following Belzrak's footsteps, which ended at the trunk of a pine large enough to carve a home out of. Belzrak dipped his head in the direction of the tree. "Here we are."

The Seer's gaze ran up the side of the tree, which stabbed at the cities that passed overhead, blissfully unaware of what awaited below. Even he hadn't known until about a year ago, and he'd made it his life's work to study the world they mistakenly called home.

The pine didn't look like it held one of the keys to destroying humanity, but the Seer supposed that was why the Makers had hidden it here. He stepped to the tree and placed his hand against the ancient bark. The shadow song echoed loudly in his mind, and he listened for his master's directions. They guided him to the other side of the tree, where a knot bigger than his head twisted the bark around itself. He placed his hand against the knot and extended his will, no different from a Manirah extending a maniblade from their precious hilts.

The tree grumbled, an old man woken from an ancient slumber. The knot expanded, opening wide enough it would permit a hand to reach inside. Darkness beckoned, but the Seer stepped back, the strength of his blood insufficient for the demands of the Makers. Belzrak took his place. He drew a beautiful obsidian dagger, the blade so dark it drank the light that dared approach, and cut a thin line across his left palm. He stuck his hand in the hole of the tree and squeezed his fist, dripping blood somewhere deep into the tree's roots.

The tree groaned and rumbled. The Seer's sense of the shadow song revealed an intricate dance of powers, manipulations he hadn't known were possible. He closed his eyes to bask in the shifting forces, marveling at the strength that remained in a mere door. When he opened his eyes again, the knot in the tree expanded further, irising open, the bark and wood of the tree as malleable as mud. A door appeared, wide enough to accommodate the largest of warriors. The ground stopped rumbling, and the Seer took a hesitant step closer.

Belzrak's eyes drank in the sight, and his reverent expression reminded the Seer his companion had never dared approach the door, either. "Shall we?" the Seer asked.

Belzrak nodded, and the Seer indicated the warrior should lead the way. Belzrak would interpret the gesture as one of honoring him, but the Seer's reasons were far more pragmatic. He didn't know what other measures the Makers had taken to protect the site, and it would be better on all counts for Belzrak to explore the ruin first.

The warrior gladly led the way, vanishing into the darkness as soon as he was within the tree. The Seer followed close behind, planting each foot carefully before risking another step. Darkness swallowed him whole, and when he turned back, he saw the entrance glowing with an otherworldly brightness.

Light and shadow played tricks on his sight. The light from the door didn't penetrate the darkness that surrounded him, for he cast no shadow and the room he stood within was lit by a flat, diffuse light, not matching at all the light the door would have cast. He searched for another source of illumination, but there was none visible.

A chill ran down his spine and he hurried to follow close behind Belzrak, who had found a spiral set of stone stairs that descended deep underground. Belzrak's soft-soled shoes didn't make a sound. The Seer's heavy steps made him feel like an intoxicated cow in comparison.

They spiraled down and down, the stairwell lit by that same flat, dull light that had no source the Seer could spot. Any chance the light could have come from the door vanished as they descended into the depths. If Belzrak was discomfited by the lighting, it wasn't revealed in his silent, even footsteps.

After descending the height of a small hill, they came to a level passage. Walls of the same metal that could be found in any city or ruin stretched before them, terminating with a door of stone that looked as though it would survive the fall of a city without a scratch. The unlikely pair walked down the long passage. Paintings hung on the walls caught the Seer's attention. Despite the flat light, the colors were vivid, bright rainbows of color against the monotonous gray of the walls, floor, and ceiling.

They depicted scenes the Seer didn't know how to properly describe, for the lives of the Makers held little in common with anything he knew. One showed a gathering of men and women around the severed head of a creature the Seer had never seen before. Another showed a woman wrestling with what appeared to be a giant snake. The final in the series was of the same woman seated beside a man, books open on their laps. If he had the time to study them further, he thought he might find valuable clues to the life and death of the Makers, but that day was not today.

A panel beside the door lit up as they approached, and Belzrak pressed his bloody palm against it. The door rumbled and scraped open. The warrior turned to the Seer. "I will go no further."

The room within was as close to a holy site as Belzrak possessed.

"I'd hoped that you would join me," lied the Seer.

Belzrak's eyes darted to the dark room, revealing his temptation, but then he slowly shook his head. "I've stared down death many times, but the mysteries within were never intended to be seen by me. If you can unlock the powers within and emerge unscathed, you will have proven yourself the rightful master of the shrines."

The Seer stretched and straightened muscles unused to the simple exertion of so many stairs. He took a long look at the way they'd come, then stepped into the room. A thick, cushioned rug on the floor muffled the sound of his boots striking against the stone. The domed ceiling glittered with pinpricks of small white light, as though he stood underneath a night sky. His vision returned to normal as colors regained their former vibrancy.

The shrine stood in the center of the room, a single

piece of what looked like some mixture of obsidian and glass. It took the shape of a pillar topped with a nearly perfect cube. Though the Seer was convinced it had been created by the Makers, when he looked at it, he couldn't help but think that it had somehow been grown from the stone.

Its power drew him close, promising a conclusion to all he had worked for. He was no stranger to awe, for his own experiences with the shadow song often reminded him of his insignificance, but nothing prepared him for the shrine. His spirit, trained to sensitivity over half a lifetime of diligent improvement, failed to comprehend the full extent of the powers locked within. He'd have had better luck attempting to count the stars in the sky.

It was the power to end the world, and he reached for it without hesitation.

Mere contact with the stone did nothing, but as soon as the Seer extended the barest thread of his spirit into the stone, it came alive, lit from within by a miniature dark star. It opened itself for him, eager to reveal truths clan scholars had spent lifetimes trying to uncover. On another day, the Seer would have pried open those secrets one after the other.

Instead, he let his awareness skim across the impossibly deep depths of the shadow song, familiarizing himself with the various abilities and knowledge the stone unlocked. The treasure Belzrak had gifted him was fit for a king. It was almost a shame he might not have the opportunity to explore all that it offered him.

The shrine was one of four connected across the continent by strands of the shadow song. All conversed freely with the others, meaning the Seer could summon the power of all the stones from where he stood. He sought that ability, extending his will through the connection to all four stones. Once their combined power was under his control, he sought the source of the Song of the Engines, hunting for it deep within the world's core.

It didn't take him long to find. Though he'd severed most of his connection with the Song that had been present at his birth, he maintained enough to find his greatest enemy. His imagination and will shaped the power of the dark stones, gathering it for an assault upon the impregnable fortress that was the Engines' source. He ground his teeth together and furrowed his brow. The shadow song didn't resist him. It leaped to his command, but he was the weak link in the chain, the part that would break first.

Before the enormous energies tore his spirit into shreds, he threw the powers he'd gathered against the source. The collision of energies rippled across the continent, and although the Seer wouldn't want to be a Manirah in the coming moments, the source still burned bright near the center of the world.

The Seer's throat was dry.

He hadn't done enough.

He hadn't been enough.

Connections dropped from his awareness as he lost the will to keep all four shrines under his control. His spirit remained in contact with this one, gently skipping upon the surface of this incredible power.

The Seer stared at nothing, his great new hope dashed, defeated by his own weakness. His breath came in shuddering gasps as he mourned the loss of his dream.

A sliver of knowledge flashed like a fish striking a fly in a stream, catching his attention. Humanity lived today, but the stones still held the future in their hands. The Seer licked his lips at the thought of what was still to come, his failure suddenly a distant memory.

Compared to striking at the source, sending out the call was as easy as flipping a switch. They answered, too long denied their purpose.

The Seer smiled as he shattered the cage that had surrounded the monsters humanity had spent generations running from.

3

Kaya sensed the shadow rising a few precious moments before it brought the Manirah to their knees. Her studies and explorations had made the Song of the Engines a part of her, little different from her heart beating its steady pace or her lungs pulling in the breath that sustained her. The attack against the source rang like a gong, shaking her bones as it rattled the very core of the world. Waves of shadow spread from the point of impact like ripples across a pond.

She dropped her spirit into the Song of Underhill's Engine, as familiar as her flesh. She cocooned herself within the Song as the wave of unnatural power rushed over her. A chill spread across her skin as the shock passed, a thick cloud briefly shadowing her from the light of the sun, but she was otherwise unharmed.

The Manirah, sensitive to the Song but disconnected from their shards at the peaceful gathering, had no warning and fared worse. The shadowy wave attacked unwary spirits, bringing most to their knees. Any who had the misfortune of being connected to their shards were struck worse. Jyn and Radyn vomited out most of the feast they'd just consumed, and they were joined by Veylan.

The Singers around her suffered the worst of all. They collapsed as though struck down, clutching at their stomachs as they heaved up their meals and the ale and wine that had washed it down. Her heart went out to them, but their suffering wasn't fatal. More important by far was isolating the source of the attack, but how?

Kaya sent her spirit wandering from Underhill's Engine to others nearby, a variation of the technique that had once allowed her to flee Nightkeep. Discordant notes greeted her as she approached each new Engine, but some notes jarred harsher than others. She focused in that direction, far south of Underhill.

Her breath caught in her throat when she sensed the Engines that labored the hardest under the assault, for they were nearly as familiar to her as Underhill's. Nightkeep's three massive Engines groaned under the weight of shadow that surrounded them, but they kept the city in the air.

Kaya sent more of her spirit toward the Engine that had kept her company when everyone else had abandoned her. She slipped between the songs of Nightkeep's Singers, stealthy as a mouse creeping around a sleeping cat. She settled into the comforting Song, then extended her awareness outward.

It didn't take long to sense a powerful source of shadow, for it lingered almost directly beneath Nightkeep's three Engines. Her spirit trembled at the depth of the shadow's strength, which made the Song of any individual Engine insignificant in comparison. The shadow was connected to others like it, a web of inky blackness that rivaled the light of the Engines.

A pulse of shadow song escaped from the site, racing

outward like the blast from the last attack. Unlike the blast, it caused no disruption in the Song of the Engines, its purpose hidden from Kaya's understanding. She stretched her perception to its limit, but whatever remained to discover was beyond her ability to sense. She retreated to the relative safety of Underhill's Engine, then returned to her body and opened her eyes. What had felt like half the day to her had been little more than a few moments in the physical world.

A handful of weaker Manirah were the first to rise to their feet. Most civilians looked pale but were otherwise unharmed. They were connected to the Song, as were all living beings, but their connection was weak enough that they were largely unaffected. Her eyes sought Radyn, whose face was whiter than a sheet, but he grimaced against whatever pain he felt as he pushed himself to his feet.

She took a step toward him but was interrupted by a groan beneath her. She looked down to see Orenil trying to lever himself into a sitting position.

Kaya cursed at herself, for she'd forgotten him in her rush to find answers. She squatted beside the young Singer who'd fallen from the sky with Firestone and ended up in her heart. "You hurt?"

Orenil shook his head, sending dark locks sweeping across his forehead. "I don't think so. What was that?"

"The most powerful manifestation of the shadow song I've ever felt. It was an attack on the source. We only felt the reverberations of it."

"The source? What happened?"

"As near as I can tell, nothing. The attack wasn't strong enough to cause any lasting damage. We were lucky."

Orenil clutched his stomach with one hand while he

swept the hair away from his face with the other. "Hard to feel lucky when my stomach feels like this."

"If the attack had cracked the source, we'd have a very different set of worries."

Orenil begrudgingly accepted the point, then swore. "I'm sorry. I should be asking about you. Were you hurt?"

"No, but thanks for asking. I need to speak with Jyn. Why don't you see if there's anyone else who needs help?"

His eyes flashed, but he smothered the emotion quickly, reason overwhelming his jealousy.

Orenil was young and ambitious. He was a year older than Kaya, which made him among the youngest of Firestone's Singers: not just currently, but of all time. Not only was he already accepted as a Singer, but he was widely considered one of Firestone's best, a once-in-a-generation talent. He reinforced his natural gift with a work ethic that rivaled the Blade's. He was widely respected, and his affection for Kaya was as true as the Song.

His greatest weakness was his pride. He'd been born with gifts, but he'd worked hard to refine that valuable talent into something useful to the clan. No matter how hard he worked, though, Kaya was always ahead of him.

He envied her easy access to the Blade, which he confessed made him doubt his worth and his efforts. He would be the first to acknowledge his irrationality, but her greater status wounded his pride all the same. Blame an accident of birth or Kaya's unique upbringing, but her gift with the Song was stronger than his. It didn't make his spirit any less than hers, but it did mean she could walk up to Jyn whenever she needed.

She pushed Orenil from her thoughts as she made her way through the crowd. Magni and several other Swords had formed a defensive circle around Jyn, but they cracked their perimeter open when she approached. The Swords were pale, but were regaining their color quickly.

Jyn had his hands on his knees. She'd never so much as seen him break a sweat, and her hands trembled at the sight. Like Radyn, Jyn had always seemed larger than life, as much myth as flesh and bone. Seeing him like this, he looked…human. His agony was no surprise, as he kept more shards on his person than Radyn, but the sight was as out of place as a city falling from the sky. He looked up from his feet. "You're going to explain what that was, right?"

Kaya did, and Jyn's face turned grave as his color returned. By the time she finished, he stood as straight as a statue, his gaze fixed on the distance. "And you believe Nightkeep is involved?"

"I can't say for sure, but it's hard to believe it wouldn't be."

Jyn swore under his breath. "Just when I thought we might have earned a break, too. Fine. I'll gather the others, and we'll meet in Underhill to decide what to do."

KAYA WAS among the first to leave after the council ended. There was only one decision Jyn could have made, and the only reason he'd convened a council at all was to involve their guests and offer them an opportunity to participate. Had Jyn been forced to solely rely on her word, Firestone and Underhill might have investigated the attack alone, but every Manirah had been struck. Their allies were frightened enough to pledge a dragon apiece. They were going to fly back to their cities and return the next morning.

Orenil, who'd been waiting outside the closed doors, stood as she exited. "What did they decide?"

"There's going to be an investigation. Jyn is sending several of our dragons, and our allies will join us."

"Good. I imagine you'll be going. Do they have any need for more Singers?"

Kaya turned left at the next intersection. The familiar hallways constricted and lengthened, squeezing her until it felt as thought the breath would never return to her lungs. She needed clear skies and an endless horizon, and she turned again, seeking the main exit. "I'm not sure. You'll have to ask Jyn."

Orenil's face fell. "I'd like to help if I can."

They walked through the open doors and into the early evening of the harvest feast. Shadow's attack had squeezed the joy out of the gathering. A few hearty souls, or perhaps just those too stubborn to acknowledge the truth of the day, remained at the tables, mugs raised in various toasts. Most, though, had finished their meals and started to clean up.

Kaya paused at the sight, the full impact of the attack hitting her for the first time. She watched Miranda, who'd spent almost every waking moment of the past week planning the festivities, direct the clean-up. She'd worn a grin this morning, but now her shoulders slumped and her voice was weary. Kaya nodded at Underhill's leader. "Perhaps you should lend her a hand. She looks like she would welcome a friendly face."

Orenil squeezed her hand. "If you don't mind me saying, you seem like you could use one more."

Kaya offered him a wan smile. "I'll be fine, although I appreciate your concern. I think I just need a little time alone."

"You're sure?" Orenil asked.

"I'm sure. Thanks."

Orenil left, glancing back twice as he made his way to Miranda's side. Kaya turned away and wandered. Her feet chose her path, and when she finally looked up, she realized she was halfway up the side of the mound that served as Underhill's domed roof. She made no effort to leash her thoughts, letting them wander as her feet had wandered. She stared at nothing in particular, but noticed when Radyn emerged from the main exit and climbed the mound until he stood behind her. He said nothing, for she knew what he would ask, and he knew that she knew.

"We'll be passing very close to Nightkeep," she said.

Radyn made a soft grunt. "You sure you want to come?"

"I don't think 'want' has much to do with it. I don't trust any of the other Singers to be sensitive enough if you run into problems. As far as I know, no one else even sensed the attack coming."

"We could find a way if we had to. You don't have to force yourself if you're worried about what we might run into."

It was a kind offer. Radyn knew better than almost anyone what Nightkeep represented. It was her childhood home, but no fond memories remained. Like almost all children, her upbringing had moments of light and love and periods of darkness, but her last years with her father had erased the memories of all that was good. He'd become obsessed with developing her abilities surrounding the Song, though to what ultimate purpose she still wasn't sure. Until today, she'd assumed Nightkeep had wanted her as a weapon against the other cities. Now she wondered if they hadn't hoped she would have some ability with the shadow song as well.

She shook her head, both in response to Radyn's offer

and to banish her own thoughts. She couldn't guess at her father's true intent, and even less the intent of the masters he had served. "I can't run from Nightkeep forever. Maybe this is the sign I should turn around and face it."

"Whatever happens, I'll be there to protect you, even if I'd rather be here."

"I know, and I thank you for it. I'll hold out hope that I don't need to confront my father, but if I do, having you by my side will mean the world to me."

They stood together in silence for a moment; then Radyn dipped his head toward the citizens cleaning up the afternoon's festivities. "Having you by his side means the world to him, too, I think."

He made the observation with a smile on his face.

Kaya sighed. "I know. I like him. Maybe even love him, but I lack the clarity of feeling he has."

Radyn offered a noncommittal grunt, which brought a hint of a smile to Kaya's face.

"Can I confess something?" she asked.

"Of course."

Kaya watched as Orenil picked up a pair of chairs and said something to a trio of young girls that had them giggling loud enough for her to hear. "I fear that I don't know my heart well enough. I don't want to promise him anything I can't back with my whole heart, but I'm afraid that in the time it takes me to sort through my feelings, he'll find someone else."

Radyn didn't answer for some time. "I don't think I'm the one to ask. Aria has always had a better grasp on matters of the heart than me."

"Then it seems to me you're the one I need to talk to, because I also lack that grasp. I understand the Song better than I understand people."

"I don't know that I have a good answer to give you.

The only suggestion I can give is to let truth guide you. If you don't think there's a future for the two of you, then say that. If you come to regret that decision three months from now, tell him that, too. Our hearts don't run in straight lines, but so long as you're honest, I don't think you'll end up regretting much."

"How did you know you loved Aria?" Kaya asked.

Radyn scratched the back of his neck and grimaced. "There wasn't any one moment. I don't even remember actually falling in love with her. We spent a lot of time together, and then one day I realized I wanted to see her every day for the rest of my life. Love snuck up on me so quietly I didn't even realize I was in danger until it was too late."

"That's my fear, too—that I won't understand myself until it's too late."

"If I were to ask you, right now, what you wanted, what would you say?"

Kaya interrogated her heart and found the answer wasn't too hard to find. "I want to be beside him."

"Then that's probably your answer. Sometimes life is simpler than we let ourselves believe."

"Thank you. For this, and for the Nightkeep offer. I'm holding out hope we don't come across the city, but if we do, I'm glad you'll be close."

Radyn bowed slightly. "And I'll always try to be, as much as I can."

Kaya returned the bow, and Radyn took his leave. She watched him stride down the side of the mound, his steps impossibly light for one who shouldered so much. Then she looked to Orenil, who was throwing himself into helping Miranda the way he threw himself into anything he did.

She smiled wider at that and went down to join him.

THAT EVENING, as the sun fell behind the golden hills, Kaya and Orenil lay entwined upon her bed. His arm was across her chest, and she was running her fingers lightly up and down his arm. Almost every muscle in her body was relaxed and her mind wandered freely, sliding from thought to thought as gently as a leaf floating down a bubbling brook.

Orenil's hand brushed some hair out of her face. "You look deep in thought."

She shook her head. "Not so much. Just content, is all."

Orenil's arm tensed, then relaxed. He was thinking about the fact Jyn had told him he was needed more here. Kaya knew it without having to ask. He bit back his complaints. "I'll be here when you return."

Warmth started in her chest and spread throughout her body. She made a pleased sound in the back of her throat.

"Hmm?" Orenil asked.

"You made me think of Radyn."

It was a poor time to say as much, and he started to pull away, but Kaya held his arm in place and explained. "He'll never say it, but he doesn't want to go tomorrow. He'd rather stay here with Aria. You're making me understand how he feels."

Orenil relaxed and shifted closer, running his fingers through her hair. "You mean that, don't you?" Not questioning or doubting, but asked in awe.

She was just as surprised to find she'd spoken true. "I do. I know you'd never ask, but I don't want to give up the study of the Song, and every long day, I want this. A home to come back to."

He brought her hand to his lips and kissed it.

"You'll have it," he promised.

4

Radyn put away the last of the chairs and tables as a favor to Miranda, and when the furniture had been returned to where it belonged, he spoke briefly with her. "Sorry it ended the way it did."

The older woman wasn't one for tears, but as she looked around the empty field, he thought he caught one of her eyes glistening. She sighed and said, "Perhaps we have no right to ask it, but just once I'd like to feel as though the future is ours. I came close today, for a bit."

"It will be ours."

"How can you be certain?"

Radyn shook his head. "I'm not. The future is a mystery beyond my understanding. But the Song has taught me faith."

"Maybe I should have become a Singer."

Miranda had never had the sensitivity to reach a level greater than Dagger. "If you'd tried, we'd have none of this, and Firestone would likely be destroyed. So though the day may seem dark, I mean it when I say that I'm honored to be working alongside you."

Miranda swallowed hard and nodded. "Thanks."

He let her be, re-entering Underhill and making his way through the labyrinthine passages to find his and Aria's apartment. The place had a much different feel than it had when he'd first settled. Firestone's residents had filled the apartments that had once stood empty, and there was a nearly constant bustle through hallways that had once echoed with the sound of his footsteps.

He found Aria on the floor, legs sprawled out in front of her. She read a book with one hand while eating an apple with the other. She greeted him with a smile as he kneeled next to her. "I assume Jyn decided to investigate the attack?"

"Not really much of a choice. We're leaving at first light."

She knew him too well to miss the hesitation in his voice. "What's wrong?"

Radyn gestured at her stomach. "Doesn't seem right to be leaving you when our family will be growing soon."

She put down her book and rubbed her stomach with her hands. Then she reached out, took his hand, and placed it on her belly. The baby kicked and Radyn smiled, his heart burning with pride. Their child hadn't even escaped the womb yet, and he thought it was the greatest child ever conceived.

"I'll miss you, too, and yes, I wish that you could stay, but you have to go for the very reason you want to be here. The best way you can protect our child is by protecting Underhill, which means finding out what attacked us."

Her reasoning was, as usual, unassailable. "Doesn't mean I have to like it."

She pulled him in for a kiss, and for a time, the rest of his worries slipped away.

He joined a handful of other Manirah the next morning in the crisp autumn air and called for Tanwen. With Firestone grounded, the clan's dragons had taken to nesting in the hills and valleys that bordered Underhill.

Macken, Firestone's former keeper of the dragons, had protested the change, but the dragons had followed Tanwen's lead without the need for much encouragement, and it had been deemed for the best. The clan's focus on preparing to survive the coming winter took all its energy, and the dragons were more than capable of caring for themselves. The dragons still came when summoned, which had sealed the decision for Jyn.

Dark shapes appeared on the horizon, wings spread wide as the dragons slowed and came in for a landing. Seven dragons in total, most of which would carry two warriors. They landed in the field beyond the boundaries Kaya and Aria had established earlier that year so that the Singers on duty in Underhill wouldn't be overwhelmed by the arrival of so much strength.

Radyn bowed to Tanwen, who'd subtly changed over the past few years. He'd grown large and complacent during his service to Firestone, but a wilder, more natural life suited him well. Lean muscles with impossible strength were barely contained under the coat of scale that protected him from the few predators that preyed upon dragons. His eyes blazed, and Radyn grinned to see his friend. "We have a long flight today with a good chance of a fight at the end. Ready?"

Eagerness flowed through their connection, and Radyn nodded. "Good. Kaya will be the one flying today. She needs the use of her senses more than I do."

The last emotion Tanwen shared through their connection was one of joy. Radyn snorted. "Traitor."

Kaya climbed up first, followed by Radyn. He ensured his hilt was secured at his hip, and when Jyn led the way into the sky, Tanwen was among the first to follow. Powerful wings, supplemented by the Song of the Engines, carried them into the clear blue. They leveled off at a height that would just carry them over the highest of hills, then worked their way south.

"Have you sensed anything from the shadow song since yesterday?" Radyn asked. He hadn't slept well the night before, a combination of pre-battle nerves and the fear that at any moment he'd be struck down by another unexpected attack. The morning's activity had reduced that fear, but couldn't quench it completely.

He'd learned how to fight against the enemy standing before him, learned how to manage the fear that came as he fought against a maniblade strong enough to slice through steel as though it was a sheet of paper, but the fear yesterday had planted in him was a different beast. Kaya said connecting to his shards and Firestone's Engine should protect him, but he wasn't so sure. Firestone's Engine still lived, but barely, a flicker of light from what had once been a raging bonfire. Most of Kaya's days were spent coaxing it back to life. She'd seen success, but claimed to be weeks away from bringing it back to full power. Underhill's Engine was still far stronger, but they hadn't started cutting shards from it yet, much less crafting hilts.

That decision, made out of an abundance of caution this past summer, felt shortsighted now, but their course had been set, even if it meant they rode into battle with the barest of protection.

"I haven't sensed anything from the shadow song, though I'm not sure that I'd sense any mundane workings.

It needs to be either close or powerful. Nightkeep hasn't moved from the spot, though."

Radyn gripped Tanwen more tightly. Other cities had answered Firestone's call for aid when it had fallen, sharing desperately needed resources they could barely spare. Nightkeep, the largest of the cities, had remained silent. He looked to Jyn, flying with Magni on the lead dragon, and hoped the Blade had some plan for when they located the source of the shadow song. They weren't nearly strong enough to fight Nightkeep alone, much less Nightkeep if it had allied itself with the shadow song.

The dragon's flight carried them up and over hills, and when Radyn grew tired of his thoughts, he watched the ground below. He tapped Kaya on the shoulder and pointed down. She had to lean over and squint, but when her eyes widened, Radyn knew she'd caught sight of them. "That's more banti than I've ever seen in one place."

"Same. And they're all heading north."

The friends watched the herd from the safety of Tanwen's broad back. So many banti made the grass ripple like waves across an enormous lake. Radyn's throat tightened at the sight, for the longer he watched, the more certain he became the banti weren't migrating north or hunting prey.

They fled something to the south.

With Tanwen traveling in the opposite direction of the banti, the sight didn't last long, and Kaya's attention returned to the dangers before them. Cut off from any sense of the Song, Radyn dwelled on what he'd seen, his imagination eager to create scenarios that froze the blood in his veins. It was easy to dismiss the herd as a small thing from up high, but he hadn't known the banti could gather in such numbers, and the sight reminded him how little they knew about this world they called their home.

His knuckles turned white as he clutched Tanwen's scales.

Wind whipped across his face as he turned to face forward. Countless miles passed underneath, and they covered in mere moments distances that would take Radyn a quarter of the day to walk.

The sun was still high when the skies to the south darkened. Enormous thunderclouds billowed high, beautiful from a distance but dangerous up close. Lightning flickered through the clouds and stabbed at the ground below, shadowed by a veil of rain. He leaned forward so that he could speak into Kaya's ear. "How close are we to Nightkeep?"

She tilted her chin toward the clouds. "They're somewhere in there, if I had to guess."

The twist in Radyn's stomach tightened as they approached the storm. The clouds reached too high to fly over, which meant that any advance would require them to fly through the heart of the storm. The dragons' senses were sharp enough to prevent collisions, but the passengers who weren't connected to the dragons would be as good as blind. The clouds, rain, and wind would help prevent Jyn's flight of dragons from being spotted, but that dagger had two sharp sides. They wouldn't see any approaching dangers either.

Jyn's dragon slowed so that it fell back beside theirs. The Blade shot Kaya a questioning look, and she nodded, pointing ahead to the storm. Jyn grimaced, then nodded back. He gave the signals for the dragons to lose some of their altitude, gather closer together, and fly into the storm.

Kaya guided Tanwen into the tighter formation as the veil of rain approached. They bled off some of their speed so the rain wouldn't lash so hard against their faces, then entered the storm. Cold rain stung Radyn's face, and both he and Kaya crouched lower, taking some meager measure of protection from Tanwen's enormous neck and head. That did little to keep them dry, and it wasn't long before their clothes turned into soaking rags. A shiver ran down Radyn's spine, and he wished he could connect with the shards in his body, for no greater reason than to keep himself warm.

Radyn leaned to the side and squinted, searching for any sign of Nightkeep. Rain obscured his vision. Jyn and the other riders in the lead were little more than dark outlines that occasionally grew sharp as they passed through the smallest of breaks in the storm, then faded again as the rain increased. Lightning cracked around them, blinding them as it lashed against the forest below.

Radyn leaned forward to ask how close Nightkeep was, but before he could speak, a bolt of lightning flashed several miles ahead of them and revealed a monster. He squinted and leaned farther forward. "Did you see that?"

Kaya shook her head.

Lightning flashed behind them, and then once again ahead, and again the shape was visible. The lead riders saw it, too, for they banked hard away.

"Is that…" Kaya's voice trailed off even as Tanwen followed the other dragons, banking away from the threat.

"A nuddu? Yes, it is."

Radyn had thought he was cold before, but a glance at the nuddu had turned his blood into a frozen sludge that crawled unwillingly through his veins. His heart pounded with the effort, so loud he feared the nuddu would hear.

Kaya twisted her head so she could keep an eye on the threat, though it had once again been covered by the veil of rain and shadow. Her disbelief kept any panic at bay. "That can't be possible. We're too far north. Even Nightkeep is too far north."

As much as he wished he did, Radyn had no answer to Kaya's objection. Nuddu had never been spotted in this part of the world, or at least, not for as long as the Singers had kept records of their travels. For as long as humanity had been confined to the sky, the nuddu had only wandered a narrow band of land that had once been the home of the Makers. He couldn't begin to guess why that wasn't true today, but there was no denying what was before them.

They were creatures that defied any meaningful comparison. Nuddu were enormous and amorphous creatures of shadow. They could stretch as high as a mountain or collapse and cover a field. When Radyn had seen one last, back when Firestone had flown through the airspace surrounding an abandoned Maker city, it had taken a vaguely humanoid shape, which wasn't much different than the shape the lightning had illuminated ahead.

Radyn, and all of humanity, knew next to nothing about the nuddu. It was often said it was the appearance of the creatures that had forced the Makers to build the floating cities, to flee the advance of the monsters, but whether that was truth or legend, no one knew. They didn't know what the nuddu ate or what sustained them. They didn't know how to kill one, or if the nuddu even died. The nuddu lumbered about slowly enough that a city could outrun them with little difficulty, but every Manirah was taught not to get too close, for it was rumored to be able to reach out quickly and catch unwary warriors.

The only other fact they knew about the nuddu was that they were attracted to the Song of the Engine, so if a city was near, the nuddu would pursue.

Jyn signaled the others that he was going to land his dragon, and he found a small plateau that would fit the entire flight. Tanwen landed softly next to Jyn's dragon, and all the riders dismounted. They were a sorry sight, covered in wet clothes that clung to their skin and chilled their limbs. Only Jyn seemed somehow impervious to the elements, standing tall against both the storm and the nuddu.

From their vantage point, they could see the vague outline of the shadowy monsters, their impossibly tall forms three times as high as the plateau the riders shared. The song wasn't strong enough in them to attract the nuddu, which was a detail Radyn's mind latched onto. Where were they going?

Kaya said, "They're heading toward Underhill."

Jyn watched the monsters for a moment longer. "I fear you're right." His frown deepened. "But didn't you say that Nightkeep is close?"

Kaya pointed south, not far from the direction the nuddu had come from. "All three cities are that direction. Maybe ten or so miles away."

Radyn picked up on Jyn's confusion. "And you can still hear their Engines?"

"As clearly as ever," Kaya confirmed.

"The nuddu walked past them without destroying them?" Radyn asked.

Kaya shrugged. "It seems that way. I'm reasonably sure Nightkeep hasn't moved since I started listening to their song, but I can't be certain. They might have evaded and returned."

Jyn wasn't convinced. "Even so, the cities of Nightkeep are much closer than Underhill. Everything we know about the nuddu tells us that it should be Nightkeep in danger."

"Everything we think we know," Kaya corrected the Blade, "but yes, it makes no sense."

Jyn fixed Kaya with a penetrating stare. "You can't hear anything in the Song that might explain it?"

Kaya shook her head, and Radyn was struck by her maturity. She was the youngest among them, but she spoke confidently to the Blade, sure of her senses and ability. She'd come a long way from the terrified girl he'd once rescued from those who sought to use her power as their own.

Jyn stood in silent contemplation as the vague shapes of the wandering nuddu vanished behind the veil of windswept rain. Then, with a long sigh, he said, "We continue our task."

Radyn was the first to object. "We can't ignore the nuddu. If they're heading toward Underhill, we need to protect our people."

"How?" Jyn challenged. "More knowledgeable warriors than us have tried, and we know no way of defending against a nuddu. Any answers, if there are any, are ahead of us. Perhaps Nightkeep has found a way to hide from the nuddu, or otherwise protect themselves. Maybe the answer to the unusual behavior is found in the shadow song, and by attacking it, we protect our people. Our only chances are ahead."

Radyn took a threatening step toward Jyn. "We can't simply abandon our people."

Jyn wasn't intimidated by Radyn's posture. "You know that isn't my intent. I'm saying that our only chances are ahead, not behind. Unless you have some sort of plan to save Underhill from the nuddu."

Thoughts and ideas tumbled over one another, but in the end, Radyn was forced into a corner. "I don't."

The matter was as good as settled then, and the riders made for their dragons, but Radyn stopped them again.

"At the least, we should send one rider back to warn Underhill."

Jyn considered the proposal, then nodded. The order was given to one of the Swords to return to Underhill. The other Sword who'd been on the dragon joined Kaya and Radyn on Tanwen, as they were the lightest of the pairs. One rider took off and raced north. The others raced south, their mission now more desperate than before.

5

Kaya closed her eyes and trusted to Tanwen's senses. The dragon handled the rain better than she could, his sense organs more attuned to the rigorous demands of flight. She pressed her face against the warmth of his scales, stealing comfort from the power of the song that resided within the dragon's chest. Through him, she felt everything with a clarity she often envied.

Though she had no wings of her own, she could feel the wind whipping past them, and she possessed the intuitive knowledge of flight. She knew how to bend her wings as the wind changed direction, how to seek the pockets of air that helped her to rise without effort. And she knew how to shape the strength of the Song to aid nature's process, to provide the lift the wings alone couldn't create.

It would be easy to immerse herself in the glory of flight, to lose herself in communion with Tanwen. Never more so than now, the melody of Nightkeep's three Engines pressing against her senses. Once, those Engines had soothed her in the same way Tanwen's song comforted her now. They had called her home and assured her that no matter the trials she faced, they would protect her. She still loved Nightkeep's Engines, for they were unlike any other, so long in unison that they had learned to harmonize and interact with themselves, weaving a rich tapestry that no single Engine, no matter how beautiful, could match.

She'd never blamed the Song for all that had befallen her, never wished that her gifts would be taken away from her in exchange for normalcy. The blame had always been her father's, his and the Singers whom he followed. Even now, only miles away from Nightkeep, closer than she'd been in years, she longed to return to those Engines. She called Underhill home, but it lacked the childhood memories Nightkeep's Engines evoked. Despite fleeing from Nightkeep, the flying city still called to her in a way Underhill never could.

It would be easy to turn Tanwen toward Nightkeep, to return home and let her future follow what path it may. Neither Radyn nor the other Sword could stop her short of killing her, and they wouldn't, no matter what she did.

The temptation faded as she sensed the other song, the shadow song, not far from Nightkeep. It came from the surface, a soft silence that hid between the notes of the Song of the Engines. It pulsed softly, too gentle to cause the chaos that she suspected it was guilty of. She wouldn't be fooled, for there was incredible power hidden within that silence, waiting to be unleashed.

She urged Tanwen lower and away from Nightkeep. They were close enough now that on a clear day they'd certainly be spotted, but the rain that covered the advance of the nuddu protected them, too. Still, there was no need to wander too close, for there would likely be dragons on patrol. If, as she suspected, the shadow song was somehow linked to Nightkeep, it also made sense to believe that dragons may be flying to and from the surface.

She took the lead, Jyn nodding her forward as she passed, and she banked so that they'd avoid Nightkeep and any dragons transiting between the city above and the ground below. Nightkeep lay slightly to the west of the site, and so they approached from the east.

The land below would be unpleasant to traverse on foot. What had appeared to be mere forest from up high revealed itself to be boggy wetlands covered in trees. Kaya pushed Tanwen lower, and together they searched for a place they could land without risking the dragons getting stuck. Tanwen found a promising patch of land first, not much more than a mile away from the source of the shadow song. Kaya had him circle a few times. The clearing seemed empty and no attacks rose to greet them, and so they landed. Tanwen's claws sank into the mud, but not so deeply he'd have trouble taking off.

Once the three riders had climbed off his back, Tanwen returned to the air, announcing to Kaya that he would look for more solid ground, but that he'd remain close. Kaya sent him a warning in the image of the Nightkeep dragons, and Tanwen acknowledged.

The other dragons came in one at a time and followed Tanwen's lead. It didn't take long for the entire group to be assembled. The warriors checked their weapons, and Kaya pointed west. "The source is about a mile that way."

Jyn ordered a line, placing Kaya squarely in the center. A wave of his hand sent them forward.

The bog slowed them, forcing the front of the line to pick their way around trees until they found a suitable path. The first quarter mile was the worst, until they found a raised path that was no stranger to footprints. Jyn glanced at them, then at his warriors, each of whom had noticed the tracks, too. There was no need to issue a warning, and they continued the cautious advance.

Kaya pushed out her senses, but this close, the shadow song drowned out the heightened senses the Song provided. It crawled inside her mind and threatened to hollow it out. For all her gifts, the shadow song's strength limited her to sight and sound, which struck her as meager tools for a time such as this. Unfamiliar birds called back and forth, cries of alarm warning neighbors that their home had been invaded. Something to her right splashed into the water and didn't resurface.

Mist rose from the bog and wrapped around their legs like tendrils. Each warrior stepped carefully, testing a fraction of their weight with each step before trusting it to support them. The lead Sword held up a fist to stop the advance. Kaya searched the gloom for the reason, but came up empty.

The bird calls had stopped and an oppressive silence had fallen. She connected with the shard in her hilt, enduring the discomfort of the shadow song against her senses. A bowstring thrummed, and Radyn's hand blurred like a snake leaping at its prey. Kaya blinked and found the tip of the arrow hovering less than a hand's breadth from her face. Radyn flexed and snapped the shaft in two with the hand that had caught the arrow. She nodded a wide-eyed thanks, but Radyn's attention had already returned to the ambush.

A dozen arrows streaked toward them, but the Swords were ready, slapping aside the arrows with the flat of their maniblades. One arrow slipped through the defense, burying itself in the thigh of one of Jyn's Manirah. The man fought on as though the attack was no more than the sting of a bee.

Kaya called upon Tanwen for support, and through

their connection, the dragon answered that he was already on the way.

Their ambushers might have been content to remain hidden by the bog, shooting at the invaders until their arrows ran out, but the sound of enormous wings in the distance made that plan less palatable. They emerged from the shadows, advancing with sure footsteps toward the Manirah.

She'd seen people like them before. They were the same people who had attacked Underhill and tried to flee through the caves, the same people who had lived in what was now the place Firestone's weary Engine rested. Men and women attacked together, each one long and lean. Most wore their hair long, and all were coated in the mud of the bog, making their movements more difficult to track in the long shadows cast by the tall trees.

They whooped and screamed as they advanced. Kaya's stomach turned to ice as the cacophony washed over her. She locked eyes with one of the women, who charged Kaya with her axe held high, hungry for blood. Kaya stepped back, then remembered the training Radyn had forced her to endure. She pulled the maniblade hilt from her hip and woke it.

The woman didn't make it to Kaya. Jyn and Radyn cut at her as though they were two halves of a whole, and the woman fell to their maniblades.

More warriors rose from the bog, though, dripping mud and water and filth, but when they drew their swords, the steel was sharp and gleamed as though reflecting the light of the nonexistent sun. She blinked, sure the numbers had to be some sort of illusion, for it seemed impossible that so many could have been hiding so close.

"Retreat!" Jyn called, but there was no place for them to retreat to. The path that had carried them here, empty just moments ago, was now filled with cold steel and colder stares. Jyn realized the same when he looked the way they'd come. He changed his mind quickly enough. "Call the dragons to pick us up!"

Kaya did as Jyn ordered, but a glance upward revealed the difficulty with Jyn's plan. The trees grew narrow here, meaning only one dragon at a time could swoop in. Their rescue would be piecemeal, and every successful rescue would reduce the number of defenders by two.

Then there was no more time for thought. Kaya called upon the shard in the hilt and let the power of the Song flow through her, strengthening her limbs and senses. The frenzied rush of the warriors slowed. Radyn and Jyn erupted in light, the strength within them nearly equal to a dragon. Jyn pushed east while Radyn remained close to Kaya.

The ambushers crashed against Jyn and his strongest Manirah, the cries of the attackers contrasted by the silent focus of the Swords and Daggers. Steel sang, hungry for flesh it would never consume, for the glowing maniblades of the Manirah made short work of the more primitive weapons. Jyn and Magni carved their way through a swath of warriors, maniblades flashing in the darkness. Like a pair of farmers rushing to finish a field before the falling of the sun, they cut their enemies down, nearly heedless of defense.

The ambushers fell back against the assault, their war cries transforming into shouts of panic and wails of grief. Jyn and Magni maintained their advance, maniblades daring any enemy to approach. A few did, either mad with grief or confident in their skills. None came close to cutting either of the large warriors.

Jyn controlled that section of the battlefield. His

movements blurred together and made Kaya think that her vision had gone hazy.

A sword aimed for her neck sent her stumbling backward and reminded her she was a participant in the battle, too. She lashed out with her maniblade, and the young man who'd tried to stab her blocked easily, but her maniblade cut through his weapon and through him. It was a poor cut, but the tip of the maniblade sliced through his stomach deeply enough to expose his internal organs to the air.

The young man raised his sword to strike, only then realizing it was a fraction of its original length. The movement of his core caused some of his intestines to spill out, and he looked down, eyes wide with surprise and confusion. Kaya cut again, a clean strike through the neck that mercifully ended the slow death she'd threatened.

Two women followed behind the young man, moving fast even to Kaya's shard-enhanced vision. At first they appeared unarmed, but too late she saw the darkness clasped tightly within their fists, daggers of shadow that threatened to steal not just her life but her soul, too. She raised her maniblade to defend, trusting in the weapon's longer length to keep her beyond the reach of the women.

The woman on her left reached her first, stabbing straight out with the dark dagger. Kaya slapped the attack away, but the woman kept the pressure on the maniblade, forcing Kaya to remain engaged. The second woman, unopposed, snuck well within her guard.

Kaya snapped the tip of her blade at the first woman, who stepped back and freed her from their contest of strength. The second woman still reached Kaya before she could bring her maniblade into play, cutting deep across her hip. A line of fire burned up her side, but she kept her jaw clenched and focused on cutting the second woman.

Unfortunately, the woman danced backward before Kaya could threaten her.

A maniblade flashed behind the women as they prepared to attack again. They fell with surprised looks, revealing Radyn standing there, looking much the worse for wear. His hair was matted from mud, sweat, and blood, and he staggered as the women fell. He favored his left leg, a cut across his right leg slowly leaking blood.

A glance behind him explained the reason. The number of enemies was less ahead of them than behind, but each moved like the wind through the bog, dozens of shadow weapons of various lengths in hand. Two of the Swords that had accompanied them to the bog were down and still.

Radyn turned as another two warriors advanced on him. Even with his injured leg, he moved nearly as fast as Jyn, and the two shadow warriors were hard-pressed to deal with his cuts.

Distracted by Radyn's efforts, Kaya didn't see the warrior reach her, but she felt the blow to the side of her head that buckled her knees and tilted the world on its axis. Too late, she realized she was lying in the mud of the path, the rest of the battle swarming around her. A foot buried itself in her stomach, expelling the last of the breath from her exhausted lungs.

A third warrior joined the fight against Radyn and he lost ground, his maniblade a blur barely keeping the shadows away.

Until it didn't. One of the warriors worked his way within Radyn's guard. Radyn shifted as the shadow dagger came for his gut, and it buried itself in his side. He roared as he pressed a hand to the side of the warrior's face. Light flashed between hand and face and the warrior went limp, the shadow blade vanishing from his hand.

Radyn staggered back, only to be tackled by a giant of a man who'd fought his way past Jyn and Magni. Both warriors flew off the path and into the nearby bog, disappearing into the dirty water.

A voice spoke startlingly close to Kaya's ear. "This is her. Restrain her and let's be off. The dragons will be here soon."

She sensed the movement behind her and tried to crane her neck, but a leather boot pressed against the side of her face kept her gaze firmly locked on the water where Radyn and the giant warrior had disappeared. Bubbles rose and the giant warrior emerged, shaking off Radyn's ineffectual blows.

Someone tried to jerk her arms behind her, reigniting the fire in her chest. Kaya struggled, kicking and flailing. She struck something soft and fleshy, earning a curse and a kick to the back that made her heart skip a beat. She coughed and gasped for the air that refused to enter her lungs. Her arms were once again yanked back harshly, and though she tried to fight, there were more and stronger arms resisting her attempts. Her wrists were pulled roughly together and lashed with what felt like a thin strap of leather.

Two strong pairs of hands reached underneath her armpits and hauled her to her feet.

"Hurry! The dragons are almost here."

Kaya kicked at her captors, then went suddenly limp, nearly dragging all three of them back to the ground. She tried to cry out for Radyn, but lacked the air to summon the words. She looked for him as the two men hauled her back upright. She wiggled and squirmed, relentless in her attempts to escape captivity. The dragons were close, and Tanwen would come for her. His presence grew in the back of her mind. He rushed as fast as his strength allowed.

The same voice said, "We don't have time for this."

There was movement to her side, and the last thing Kaya saw before her world descended into darkness was the giant who'd tackled Radyn holding his hands under the water, as though choking the life out of the savior of Firestone.

6

Radyn's body burned as though it had been dipped in oil and lit on fire. The wound in his side had started the inferno, the darkness eating like acid through his insides. The fire spread as he was tackled into the filthy water. His lungs joined the celebration a moment later as the giant held him down in the mud.

The pond wasn't more than a few feet deep, but that was more than enough for the giant to drown him in. Radyn had gasped and inhaled as he'd been tackled, but the precious air mattered little as he wrestled with the warrior who was twice his size. The Song of the Engines burned in his veins, but the muscles of the giant were reinforced with shadow, as strong as steel, and Radyn couldn't budge them, no matter how he fought.

The impact of the tackle had knocked the maniblade from his hand. His right hand scrambled to find the weapon, but in the mud and the muck it was as good as gone, his last reminder of Elora. He tried to form a weapon in his palm, but the burning in his chest and the lack of air in his lungs destroyed any shred of focus he could summon.

Enormous hands found his neck and squeezed tight, as though wringing water from a used rag. He gripped the giant's wrists and pulled, but he might as well have tried to rip steel apart. Panic caused him to flail, beating ineffectually against his killer's arms and torso. He clawed at the giant's eyes, but his efforts were casually batted away, one oversized hand more than enough to hold him under.

The Song grew louder: not to give him strength, but to call his spirit to the gate. It flashed before him, the pale blue glow of the Engines, but carved into the shape of an arch. It floated on an endless expanse of water that was as still as glass. Two figures sat before the gate, deep in silent conversation. They turned as one, a woman and a man, although the man's eyes glowed with a golden light. The woman frowned at him, and a voice spoke in his mind and echoed across the infinite ocean. "We weren't waiting for you."

He saw Aria before him, stomach swollen with child, and the gate receded as though he flew away at a great speed.

His lungs burned for air and his body bucked, but for a moment his mind was steady. He summoned a blade to hand and thrust it under the giant's jaw and into his brain. The crushing pressure on his throat eased, and he used the last of his strength to shove the giant corpse to the side. He heaved himself up as his body finally surrendered to his need for breath.

Air had never tasted so sweet, at least until he gagged and coughed up muddy bog water. A fit of fierce coughing left him oblivious to all except the burning pain in his side and the silt that raked the inside of his mouth. Once the fit passed, Radyn spat out bog and took in the chaos that surrounded him.

Jyn and the surviving Swords held strong against the weaker warriors who had cut off their retreat. The Song enveloped Jyn, a burning cloak of light that reminded Radyn more of a dragon than a mere man. Magni guarded Jyn's back, and if he lacked his Blade's strength, he made up the difference in sheer ferocity. Shadow warriors tripped and stumbled as they fled from his maniblade.

Had the weaker opponents been their only foes, Radyn might have rated the Manirah's chances highly. But the dark warriors who had overwhelmed him closed the noose on Jyn and the others. Jyn's massive strength wasn't sufficient. He stretched out his hand and found Elora's maniblade close. He clutched it tight and pushed himself to his feet.

Only to find himself back on his rear, gasping in pain. Spasms wracked his body, and he wrapped his arms around his core, willing the pain to fade. It wasn't a foe so easily overwhelmed, though. He breathed through clenched teeth and looked for Kaya.

The girl was nowhere to be found. He couldn't see her body on the path, but she wasn't with Jyn and the others. He'd been right ahead of her. His eyes darted up and down the path, stopping when he caught motion to the west. A group of warriors retreated, and one carried a corpse over his shoulder. He leaped over a tree limb and the corpse stirred.

Kaya.

Pain faded against the advance of desperation. Radyn sucked in his breath, ground his teeth together, and stood. Flames of agony speared through his side, but his legs supported his weight on a wobbly foundation. His vision swam, and it was all he could do to keep his balance. The strength of the Song kept him upright, but he could feel it waning.

A glance back at Jyn revealed little new, but his presence in that battle made no difference one way or the other. He turned his back on his fellow Manirah and shuffled and stumbled back to the path. He slipped in the mud and barely kept his balance. Then he was on the path and stumbling forward, forgotten by both the shadow warriors retreating and those drawn to Jyn like moths to a flame.

Jyn's control over the Song grew brighter yet, which should have been impossible. Too curious not to turn, Radyn watched as dragons descended from the sky. The first flew over the battle, a whirlwind of bloodstained claws and teeth as sharp as a maniblade. She fell among the shadow warriors, granting the surviving Manirah a moment's respite. Jyn's dragon dropped in behind the first, scooping the Blade and Magni in his massive claws with the gentleness of a child picking a flower. One powerful beat of his wings, strengthened by the Song, shot the dragon and his passengers into the sky faster than an arrow.

Radyn watched long enough to ensure Jyn was safely away, then turned his attention back to the matter of pursuit. Those Swords that had survived this long would live for the next fight, as they'd trained diligently in the art of fleeing a hostile battlefield. His thoughts were only for Kaya. Tanwen remained in the back of his mind, meaning it was as good as certain that Kaya had been knocked unconscious. The dragon circled overhead, hidden from sight by the low clouds. Radyn shuffled forward, imagining a plan in which he and Tanwen worked together to free Kaya. He could ask the dragon to swoop in and scatter the warriors he'd just seen, then recover Kaya before the shadow warriors regained their composure.

The warriors moving west, in the direction of the shadow song, didn't so much as look behind them. Did they not care about the outcome of the battle with Jyn, or were they simply so confident in their superiority they considered the outcome as good as sealed? Regardless of the reason, Radyn thanked them for not spotting him, for he lacked the strength to hide.

His lungs and legs burned as he hauled himself through the wet mud of the path. His steps squelched, and if he wandered too close to the edge of the path his feet would sink, the mud gripping up to his ankles in an attempt to pull him down.

He wasn't gaining on the group. He summoned more strength from the shards scattered throughout his body, but their answer only added fuel to the fire that burned up his side. The strength of the Song knew no limits, but Radyn's body had surpassed its shortly after the ambush began.

He focused on Kaya's limp form and gritted his teeth through the pain. He gripped his maniblade tighter and imagined Elora by his side, urging him forward. It was Kaya who might one day learn how to heal the Engines for good, Kaya who might save them all. His skill with a maniblade was nothing in comparison.

A shout from behind forced him to turn around. The shadow warriors had begun their return, disappointed their enemies had fled. Spotting Radyn sparked a bloodlust that hadn't yet cooled, and they charged, steel and shadow seeking his head.

Radyn half-shuffled and half-ran, but his attempt to put distance between them was doomed before it began.

His injury slowed his steps and the constant pain shredded his focus, but still he pursued the Singer who was nearly a daughter to him.

He tripped and almost fell, but regained his balance. Another lance of pain shot up his side and he bit back a curse. He shuffled to a stop. His legs wobbled and his breath came in ragged gasps. The small horde of shadow warriors closed the distance, racing each other to see who could land the first and possibly final blow against him.

Radyn stared at the back of Kaya's head, bouncing along as she was carried, then closed his eyes and searched for any scrap of strength that remained. He ended his search empty-handed, and his shoulders sagged. He called for Tanwen, who was close.

Radyn turned and clipped the maniblade to his belt, and watched as Kaya's captors shifted direction and slipped behind a wide tree. The heart of the shadow song was close as it pressed against Radyn's senses. He caught another glimpse of Kaya and her captors, and then they were lost to the trees and the bog and the mysteries ahead.

A hastily thrown spear landed in the mud several paces behind Radyn, signaling the imminent arrival of his enemies. He didn't bother to face them as Tanwen's presence grew ever larger in his mind. His old friend swooped over the heads of his enemies, claw and tooth dispersing the assembly, then picked Radyn up like a child recovering a lost toy.

Radyn twisted his head so that he might once again catch sight of Kaya, but neither she nor her captors were anywhere to be found. The outline of the path was visible, his pursuit easy to spot, but of the others there was no sign.

"Can you sense her?" he cried.

Tanwen replied that he could, and in Radyn's mind's eye, he saw images of tunnels too tight for a dragon.

Radyn cursed loudly. Whatever slim threads of hope for the future Underhill and Firestone had grasped, they were cut now. Kaya was gone, and with her, his dreams of the future.

And he had been the one who lost her.

7

Kaya woke in a small room lit by a single lantern. Every beat of her heart made her head feel as though a powerful carpenter hammered nails into it, and her vision swam as she lifted her face to look around. She closed her eyes and squeezed her lips shut so that she wouldn't groan and let her captors know she was awake.

When the wave of nausea passed, she cracked open her eyes. She was seated on a rough wooden chair. Her wrists were bound behind her back, then tied to some part of the chair she couldn't see. Another strap had been wrapped around her torso, but it was loose and felt more like an afterthought, as though she'd been in danger of slipping out of the chair. Her ankles were tied to the legs of the chair, securing her firmly in place. The door to the room looked thin enough to be split by a strong breeze, but it might as well have been one of the steel doors guarding the Engine at Underhill for all the good it did her.

She closed her eyes again to calm her racing heart. Panic crept around the edges of her awareness, barely kept at bay through a focus on her breath. She listened for the

Song of the Engine, seeking refuge in the melodies and harmonies that she knew as well as her own scars.

The Song was silent.

Her heart skipped a beat and threatened to flee from her chest. The Song couldn't be silent, for it was the Song of life. The fact that her heart still beat and her breath came in shallow gasps meant the Song continued. She'd just been cut off from it, a limb amputated without her consent.

Kaya stretched out her senses and sought the familiar melodies, its absence more frightening than her captivity or the advance of the nuddu. She didn't make it far. Strands of the shadow song were wrapped around this room like a net, she a fish plucked from the lake. It wasn't a perfect net. With focus, she thought she might find a gap and reach for the Engines, but the pounding of her head and the aches of her body made focus a distant goal.

Footsteps outside her door made her tremble. She looked from side to side like a squirrel that could somehow escape its fate. Voices spoke low, and one was familiar, a voice from her past a part of her had hoped to never hear again. She jerked at her bonds, but they offered no more give than they had before. The thin leather thongs cut into wrists already burned raw from her capture and transport.

The door opened, and her father stepped in.

Kaya's body went limp, every scrap of strength pulled from her with just a single glance from Father. The darkness that had once hidden in his shadow now pulsed in his veins, claiming what little good she remembered his spirit possessing. His face expressed concern, but the shadows in his heart danced with glee.

He didn't rush to embrace her. Didn't cut her bonds and pretend to be her savior. He couldn't even bring himself to say her name. He pulled a second chair into the room, as roughly carved as the first, then settled his bulk on it.

Father had grown outward since she'd seen him last, the additional flesh hanging loosely. His face was rounder, but his eyes had lost none of the cruelty she remembered all too well. His once lustrous hair had dulled and turned gray, and though he'd once been fastidious about his appearance as a Nightkeep Singer, those days appeared to be deep in his past. Light from the lone lantern was reflected in his dark gaze, then flickered and died.

She was a child again, a solitary spark of light surrounded by a darkness that encroached upon all that was good. The Song was life, was the fundamental nature of the world, but the darkness consumed it. Ice gathered in her chest and she almost cried out for forgiveness, the same as she had so many times when she was younger.

Kaya blinked and remembered herself. Father wasn't the only one who had changed in the years since she'd escaped Nightkeep. She imagined Radyn beside her, unable to help, but sharing his courage. She sat up as straight as her bonds allowed and met Father's eye.

"It's been a long time," he said.

His presence gave her fears a focus, and that focus brought the softest hints of the Song to her senses. No matter how dark the day, the Song remained, a reminder that hope only died if she let it.

Venom coated her tongue, the desire to lash out almost unbearable. It would be pointless, though. His spirit had traveled to a place where her words couldn't touch him. Unleashing her frustrations would do her no more good than shouting at a wall. She pressed her lips together and observed, the way Radyn had taught her.

He fidgeted in his chair as she waited for him to respond, and it was his gaze that fell first to the floor of her cell. She was captured and bound, wrapped in a net of shadow, and still he was afraid of her. For all that had changed between them, some remained the same. He looked up, saw her steady gaze, and growled. "Your friends abandoned you."

She remembered Radyn's desperate fight against overwhelming numbers. "Abandonment" was hardly the right word, and if Jyn and the others had fled from the ambush, she held no bitterness in her heart, only gratitude they'd escaped with their lives. Far from turning her against the warriors who were closer to her than blood, Father's words strengthened her resolve. The odds they knew she was alive and captured were slim. She couldn't rely on anyone else to rescue her.

Fair enough. She'd only been awake a short time, but she longed to see the others again. To share her bed with Orenil again.

When she still didn't respond, her father stood and shoved the chair into the corner of the room. "All these years, and you have nothing to say to your father?" He raised a hand as though he might slap her, but froze before he could strike. He glanced around the room, wary eyes darting from shadow to shadow. His hand fell and he straightened the creases in his clothes. He still wore the garb of a Singer of Nightkeep, robes white and immaculately clean. The robes that lended a sense of sacredness to other Singers only made him look vain and empty.

Father grabbed the chair and sat back down. "I'm sorry. Perhaps it may not seem like it from your perspective, but I have only ever tried to do what I thought was best for you. Discipline can be hard for a child to understand."

He was too lost in his monologue to witness the venom

in her glare. He knew nothing of discipline or sacrifice, nothing of the Song or its mysteries. The Song had gifted him an unusual sensitivity, strong enough to allow him to pass the trials that allowed him to sing to Nightkeep's Engines, and he'd seen nothing but a path to wealth and leisure.

"But now my wayward child has returned to the fold, and just in time, too. The future of humanity rests upon a precipice, and your gift may be exactly what we need."

He finally paused and waited for her to respond, to ask anything of him, but she held on to her silence. He snarled, then schooled his face to serenity. "You were always a disrespectful brat. I gave you everything, and in return, you fled."

She stared at her father in amazement, for he spoke with conviction. He believed the words that leaped so easily from his lips.

He'd given her everything? It was true she'd grown up the child of a Singer in the wealthiest city in the world. She'd never worried about where her next meal would come from, or if it would nourish her body. She'd enjoyed the tutelage of some of Nightkeep's greatest scholars.

But she'd also been ignored within the walls of the apartment. When she wasn't being trained or taught, she was expected to be silent, out of sight and out of mind, so that Father could either find himself a new wife or hatch whatever schemes that week brought. If she dared seek his company, she was rewarded with slaps and shouts, and more often than not was locked in her bedroom for the rest of the day and night. In the morning, when he unlocked the door, he made her bow, head to the floor, and apologize for bothering him. He was a great man, too busy to be bothered to fulfill a child's desire to play.

Once she'd asked if she could just play with others, but

that, too, was out of the question. Her gift with the Song was already apparent, and Father's plans included her. She wasn't supposed to mingle with the rabble that would only serve to distract her.

There'd been a month or two, after Father had remarried, that life had taken a turn for the better. Kaya knew now it was only because Father had been uncertain of his new wife's temperament, but when he understood she was every bit as ambitious as him, and equally callous to Kaya's desires, the situation turned worse than before. She was restricted to her room whenever she wasn't training or learning. Those were the days when Kaya had first learned to sense the shadow growing long throughout Nightkeep's hallways.

Yet here he sat, oblivious as ever, convinced he was the victim.

She was no stranger to false beliefs. Everyone, herself included, fell prey to them. The depth of Father's conviction, contrasted with the sheer wrongness of his belief, tightened the knots in her stomach until she thought she might vomit.

Radyn's training saved her. She latched her awareness onto her breath, centering her attention and turning it once again upon her father. The shadow song had its hooks deep in him, far deeper than the ones she'd sensed in Jelrik months ago. How many of Father's beliefs were his, and how many were twisted and warped by the shadow song?

Untangling the two was a meaningless battle, especially now. She made no answer to his accusations, certain he would twist whatever she said to suit his means.

"Be that way," he said, standing from his chair violently enough to push it over. "I'd hoped to invite you to join us, but it's clear that more—aggressive—persuasion will be necessary. I didn't want to see it come to this, but you've brought this upon yourself, left me no choice. When the pain comes, I want you to know it was your fault, your willfulness, that caused it. I tried to save you, but you refused my kindness."

He left the room and the door was shut behind him, sealing her once again in darkness.

Panic clawed its way up through her stomach and toward her throat. Tears gathered at the edges of her vision, and she looked up so they wouldn't fall.

She returned to her breath. Her future seemed dark, but it had before, and the Song had triumphed. She had to believe that it would again.

Father had failed in whatever purpose had brought him to her, but he'd succeeded in focusing her fear. She dove deep within her spirit and sought the Song, seeking a way to free herself from the webs of darkness that surrounded her.

8

Tanwen's connection to the Song pulled Radyn's body out of mortal danger, but did nothing to close the gaping wound Kaya's disappearance had opened in his spirit. They followed Jyn and the others, circling wide around the nuddu as it relentlessly lumbered north.

Jyn was already in council with other cities' representatives when Radyn landed. Aria stood by the main entrance of Underhill, and was at Radyn's side as he half-dismounted, half-fell from Tanwen's back. She took one look at his mud- and blood-stained clothing and asked, "How bad is it?"

"I need a healer, and soon."

She wrapped his arm around her, then supported him as they walked deeper into Underhill. Radyn's strength, no longer augmented by Tanwen's spirit, fled like water from a sieve. He stumbled as the hallway twisted in his vision. Aria called his name, though she sounded a great distance away.

Strong hands grasped him, and the sudden movement pulled at the flesh around his open wound. The fire that erupted in his side returned awareness to his broken and battered body. Several Daggers had answered Aria's call, and they had mostly picked him up and were dragging him toward the healer's quarters. He searched desperately for Aria and she was there, beside them, his blood staining the new shirt she'd just sewn for herself to accommodate her growing stomach. "I'm sorry," he said.

She frowned at him. "Hush. You'll be at the healers' rooms shortly."

His brief flirtation with awareness faded, darkness again crowding the edges of his vision. "It needs to be Maisie."

Aria's frown deepened. "Why?"

He drifted away, then shook himself awake. "Get Maisie!"

The effort took the last of his strength, and the last he saw was Aria nodding before his world faded to black.

HE WOKE to Maisie's stern face above his. They'd crossed paths a few times since Firestone and Underhill had been forced into unity, but never for long. Her gray hair was turning white and her wrinkles had deepened, but her gaze had lost none of its sharp focus. She grunted as she leaned back. "You're awake."

Radyn squeezed his eyes shut and groaned. The lights of the healing ward had been turned down low but still stabbed like needles into his sensitive eyes. The Song roared around him, deafening in its volume and overwhelming in its complexity. His body was connected with each of the shards embedded under his skin through no intent of his own. Strength flooded his limbs, more than he'd ever pulled before.

"What—"

Maisie's rapid breaths echoed in his ears, and her heart beat quickly, each thump sounding like a drumbeat. He smelled her sweat.

Despite her age, she was in fine health. What nerves or excitement were causing—?

Radyn's thoughts froze. She couldn't have. She wouldn't dare.

He disconnected himself from his shards, one at a time. It took him seven repetitions to finish the task. A shudder ran through his body at the thought. He imagined grabbing her by the throat and slamming her against the wall, but she wouldn't have acted without reason.

They were alone, and no surprise that. Maisie never would have pulled such a stunt with witnesses near. He spoke in a whisper. "How dare you?"

She waited a beat, then answered. "I won't lie and say I haven't thought of this day. I've been preparing for it since Elora died. Still, I wouldn't have acted without your permission, except that I believed you might have died otherwise. The infection had spread deep within your body, beyond the reach of any healing strength I possess. When I first examined you, I could hardly believe you were alive. If not for Tanwen, I suspect you'd be waiting for Aria and your unborn child on the other side of the gate."

The glowing blue arch loomed large in his memories, but Radyn kept his thoughts to himself.

"I needed strength, and it was the only way I could acquire it for you in time."

"Seven? I should be dead."

Maisie nodded. "I agree, but your body has grown used to the Song over the years. Your prolonged exposure to the shards has changed you."

Radyn stared at the ceiling. Colors remained too vivid,

and Maisie's voice too loud. His senses were too sharp for daily living, some strength leaking from the shards even though he fought to keep his distance from them. Hopefully he'd find a way to increase the separation before he found himself in a crowd.

"Thank you," he said.

"You're welcome. You were wise to have Aria fetch me. You would have died before anyone else could have figured out what was happening in your body. How do you feel?"

Radyn sat up. He twisted his torso, grimacing as the fresh flesh complained about the use. He flexed his fists, then rolled off the table and shook his body out from crown to toe. "I can feel the lingering pain from the healing, but otherwise, better than I have any right to expect."

Maisie began packing up her scalpels and other instruments of her trade, placing them carefully into a small bag. "It will take a day or two for the pain to diminish, but I healed the skin until it was as thick as normal. You might notice a slight loss of mobility until your body fully adopts the new flesh, but I figured you needed durability more."

"Why?"

"You've been out for less than a quarter of the day. Jyn and the others are still meeting. We don't know what they're talking about, but it must be serious to keep them this long."

"There's two nuddu coming our way. They'll probably be here in the next few days."

Maisie's reaction was delightfully muted. She raised an eyebrow. "Well, I did my part by keeping you on your feet. I'll leave it to you to figure out how to stop a nuddu."

With that, she left, and Radyn shook his head.

He didn't deserve such faith, but he'd do all he could to justify it.

THE SWORD STANDING guard at the door let Radyn in without a question, and his arrival brought what had clearly been a stormy argument to a brief pause. Cups of tea had been poured around the table, but most of the council's members were on their feet, their cooling beverages long forgotten.

Every face in the room was familiar. No small number of them had been part of the attempt to defeat the shadow song. Their uniforms were as stained with mud and blood as his, and eyes rimmed with exhaustion stared at him with a hope he wasn't sure he could fulfill.

Jyn took advantage of the interruption to return to his seat. The others followed his lead. He sipped at his tea, grimaced at the temperature, and placed it gently down on the table, the cup looking tiny in his powerful hands. "Radyn, it's good to see you up and well. I heard that your injuries were severe."

Radyn bowed in response, then took an empty seat. "Thank you. Has anything been decided yet?"

Jyn took a slow look around the room. "We agree the threat is existential. We haven't yet come to an agreement on how we meet that threat."

"What options are you considering?"

"Some have suggested attacking the nuddu from the dragons; others have discussed ideas for defending Underhill. Others think we should flee, either by attempting to get Firestone back in the air or by evacuating Underhill on foot and by dragon. Unfortunately, our numbers are such that our allies still in the air can't help us.

None could absorb the numbers of refugees we'd dump on them, even if they worked together and divided us among them."

All fine ideas, as far as ideas went, and all doomed to failure. Radyn saw Jyn's acknowledgment of that lurking in his eyes. When he looked around the room, he saw it shared by everyone. They would act for the sake of doing something, but they knew.

Radyn let the silence linger for a moment, then said, "The nuddu aren't our enemy. The shadow singers are, and they've captured Kaya."

Several of the warriors shifted in their seats. Some leaned forward, while others flinched away.

Jyn raised the obvious objections. "First, we don't even know that Kaya is still alive. Second, if she is, there's no way I can think of to rescue her. They were waiting for us before and we got beaten badly. Third, even if we do somehow rescue her, there's still a pair of nuddu bearing down on us."

Radyn raised his fist, then raised one finger. "Kaya is still alive. Tanwen is certain, though he has trouble sensing her." He raised a second finger. "We attack with everyone." He raised a third finger, then shrugged and put his hand down. "To tell the truth, I'm not sure rescuing her will somehow solve our problems with the nuddu. But what I do know is that any sliver of a chance we have starts with her. Whether we seek to fight the nuddu or raise Firestone, we'll need her."

Veylan snorted. "This is madness. We'd all heard of the shadow warriors you encountered earlier this year, but none of us suspected their numbers or their strength. Charging back into that bog is madness, especially if Nightkeep has formed an alliance with whoever those warriors are. You're risking all-out war."

"War is on your doorstep. We're only asking you to choose a side," Radyn said.

Veylan rose. "Such a decision is not mine to make, and so I'm afraid I must deny your request, but even if it were up to me, I would refuse you. At the very least, Nightkeep has found a way to avoid the gaze of the nuddu. At worst, they've learned how to command the creatures. We can't afford to make an enemy of them."

"After what you've seen, you think they're interested in an alliance?" Jyn asked.

"No, but I'm not convinced they're my enemy, either."

"You're a fool if you honestly believe that," Radyn said.

Veylan shrugged. "Even if they seek to dominate us, my pride does not compel my decisions. Servitude is still survival. If that is their plan, I will not be pleased, but my oath is to protect my people, even if that means surrendering to Nightkeep's will."

Jyn stood to stand beside Veylan. "There's a possibility you haven't considered. At worst, they'll send the nuddu after you once they're done with Firestone and Underhill."

Uncertainty flickered behind Veylan's eyes, the first sign of distress he'd shown since Radyn had entered the room. He wasn't a fool, but Radyn could understand the hope for peace, misguided as it was.

Veylan met Jyn's gaze as he weighed his options. "I will convey your request to my Blade. However, it will still take at least a day and a bit to get the message to Skystone and return with an answer, and by the time we organize and arrive, I'm afraid we'd be no help. I couldn't assist even if I wanted."

Jyn bowed. "I am grateful for your efforts, regardless."

Veylan returned the bow, then swept out of the room, leaving a void larger than he was. All eyes turned to Jyn, who in turn looked to Radyn. "You really think Kaya is our only hope?"

"She knows more about the Song than anyone I've met, and she's more fluent in the language of the shadow song than I am. I can't claim any certainty she'll save us, but if we have any hope, it's with her. It's the only hope we have that's worth anything."

Magni, sitting on Jyn's right, chimed in, "I agree with Radyn. The odds are poor, but they're the only odds. We're fooling ourselves if we think there's anything else we can do against the nuddu."

Jyn gestured to the rest of the Swords gathered around the table. "I can't say I like Radyn's idea, but I have none better. I'll accept it unless someone here can convince me otherwise."

He gave them time to answer, but no answers were forthcoming.

Jyn once again turned his tired eyes to Radyn. "Then it's decided. We go to war."

9

Kaya had no real sense of time passing. This deep underground, the light from the surface was a distant memory, and no one checked on her or offered food. She was too busy with her own explorations to notice the passing of time, poking and prodding the web of shadow that surrounded the room. She'd succeeded in loosening the shadow's hold on the cell, though the difference was so little it would be meaningless to anyone but her. The Song whispered to her now, though, reminding her she wasn't alone. Not strong enough to give her the strength to put up a fight, but something.

She heard footsteps in the hallway. They weren't heavy, exactly, but ponderous, as though their owner was weighted down with heavy thoughts. As when her father had visited, there was quiet conversation on the other side of the door, then a knock, and then the door opened to reveal a man she'd never seen before.

That lack of familiarity didn't mean she couldn't identify him, though. There were others in whom the shadow song had its claws deep, such as her father. This man was something else entirely. The shadow song was in him, intertwined with his spirit in such a way that Kaya was certain that if the two were separated, the man would die. His eyes had turned black, causing her to shudder when he looked at her.

"Kaya. I have heard so much about you over the years. It's a pleasure to finally meet you in person."

His voice was higher-pitched than she expected, and nasal, too. He was a fat man, his belly as wide as his broad shoulders, but she also sensed it would be a mistake to underestimate his physical strength or speed. The shadow song gave him abilities far beyond appearances; of that, she had little doubt. His dark, matted hair was a mess and his skin pale, even for a city-dweller.

She choked back her revulsion. "I wish I could say the same."

The man took no offense at her disrespect. "Perhaps, in time, we may come to agree with one another. Yours is a special spirit and a special gift, and I'd like to believe that once you understand all that I've come to understand, you'll see the world as I do."

"I've sensed enough of the shadow song's powers. It seeks only to kill and destroy. What makes you think I'd ever see as you do?"

The Seer tsked. "Imprecise language is the root of misunderstanding. I would have thought your father would have taught you that, at least. The song I serve doesn't want to 'only kill and destroy,' as you say. It wants to restore this world to its rightful glory. To achieve that, though, humanity must perish."

"I'm not sure that I find the difference a meaningful one," Kaya said.

"But it makes all the difference in the world." The Seer stood, his motions far smoother than Kaya would have expected from a man of his size. It was like watching an oak tree pick up its roots and dance. The Seer paced the small room slowly as he said, "You might call my deeds acts of murder, but you'd be wrong. Murder is about lust and anger, jealousy and hate. It's crude and meaningless."

"But when you do it, it's not?"

"You speak in jest, but yes. My deeds are imbued with meaning, and though my story will never be told, this world will sing my praises for generations to come."

His words invited her mockery, but she could hear Radyn's warning in her ear as he trained her as Elora had once trained him. "Be on your guard diligently against judgment, for once the judgment is made, your perception is irrevocably altered."

He wasn't a leader in the same way Jyn was a leader. Jyn's physical presence and steely demeanor inspired the Manirah under his command with nothing more than a look or a gesture. Those that followed him wanted to be like him.

She couldn't imagine anyone would look at the Seer and want to imitate him. So what about him drew such dangerous believers into his midst? She didn't understand, and made no effort to hide her confusion. "Why? Why would this world sing your praises?"

A slow grin spread across his face as he again took his chair. "You really don't know, do you? All your skill with the Song, and you still haven't figured it out."

"Figured out what?"

The Seer scooted his chair closer to hers. "I'll start with the fact I learned that changed the course of my life." He paused for dramatic effect. "Humans don't belong here. This world is not for us."

He didn't make it easy to withhold judgment, but she tried. "What do you mean?"

The Seer spread his arms wide. "Humans didn't evolve on this world. We're not like the banti or the nuddu, who called this world home long before we did. We came from the stars."

Kaya stared, unable to fashion a response to justify such foolishness.

"You may not yet believe, but if you hold the explanation in your heart, I think you'll find that it makes more sense than you expect. Why is this world so eager to kill us? Because we don't belong here. We're making our homes in a place we don't own. We're a sickness inside the body the world is trying to get rid of, but there's nowhere for us to go, so we cling tenaciously to life."

"If our ancestors came here so long ago and found the world inhospitable, why didn't they simply turn around and leave?"

"I don't know."

His easy willingness to acknowledge what he didn't know shook her to her core, the difference between her expectation of him and the reality stark. Shouldn't he pretend to know everything? That casual admission did more to convince her he spoke true than any impassioned defense.

He continued. "All that I know is that they settled, and they built, and they became the people we know now as the Makers. For their invasion, they were targeted by the world, and we, their distant ancestors, now pay the price."

"And your solution is to surrender? To help us kill ourselves?"

"It is not the language I'd use, but yes."

Again, the simple admission left her mind lurching for something to hold on to. The words he spoke were as mad as any she'd ever heard, but he was so calm, so sure of himself and his ideas, so willing to admit what he didn't know. He was, in short, compelling. A raving madman she could have dismissed without problem, but this calm assault on her history, not so much.

"I take a wider view, Kaya, and though you are quick to label me a monster, I'd ask you to tilt your head just a little and look at the world with a fresh perspective. The problem is not the shadow song, or the nuddu, or the world we call home. The problem is humanity itself. You know this better than anyone. We take and take and rarely give back. Singers don't train their entire lives to understand the Song and return some of what they've taken, no. They train to manipulate the Song, to use it and bend it to their will. The Maker cities, which now lie in ruins, once destroyed the land and polluted the air. All that I'm doing is restoring balance to a world too long sent awry by our predecessors."

The Seer stood again, and Kaya had the sense that he had said almost everything he had come to say.

"Please, think on what I've said. You look at my actions through a narrow lens and call me a villain, but if you step back, I think you'll see it differently. We're just another animal, no better or worse than a deer, a spider, or a banti. It's time we step aside so that this world can return to its natural state. I love this world, and I want to see it thrive, even if that means it goes on without us. Take your time, think it through. Understanding is worth the effort."

He turned as if to go, then tapped the side of his head. "Sorry, one more thing that I'd forgotten. I've sensed you working your way through the protections I placed around this room. I don't blame you for trying to reach the Song, but it has no place here, and I'm afraid you might be addicted to it, so this is for your own good."

He placed a large hand on her shoulder, and a spear of darkness stabbed at her spirit. The thin shreds of Song she controlled protected her innermost soul, but the shadow was in her now, darkness spreading its hooks. She screamed as a burning sensation spread across her shoulder, and any trace of the Song beyond her cell vanished from her senses.

Kaya ground her teeth together so she wouldn't shout again.

The Seer bowed to her, then left, leaving her to face the darkness encroaching upon her soul alone.

SHADOW FOUGHT its way through her body, clawing and scrabbling for purchase and refusing to let go of any hard-fought terrain. Kaya gasped for air as sweat dripped down her face. More than once, the shadow surged forward, sliding deeper into her spirit like an icy snake. It ripped screams from her throat, but no relief came from the other side of the door.

She sagged against her bonds. Sleep and rest called to her, but if she surrendered to that desire now, she'd never be free of shadow. It would set its anchors in her spirit and lock itself in place. Deep breaths gave her the chance to gather her strength and focus on another attempt.

She'd displaced the shadow from Jelrik easily enough. For all its strength, shadow couldn't stand long against the Song. If only she could stretch out her will and grasp it, relief would soon be at hand. Unfortunately, this room and its isolation from the Song weakened her attempts. Her prolonged efforts bore meager fruit, though, the weaving of the shadow too complex to be surpassed in her distracted state. If she focused her will and lunged for the Song, the shadow lurking within seized advantage of the moment and consumed more of her spirit.

Three attempts left her increasingly desperate, the shadow eager to devour anything she left unguarded. At this rate, it wouldn't be long before she would be forced to surrender.

She returned, as she so often did, to the breath, the gentle flow of air from her nose to her lungs. Friends and family came and left, but her breath was a constant companion from the day of her birth to the day her spirit fled her body and passed through the gate. As she followed the breath, she followed also the flow of the Song through her body. The amount was a sliver of a fraction of what the Engines produced, but it was hers, even if she'd been excised from the greater Song.

With a steady breath and consistent effort, she fanned the flame of her spirit, guarding always against the encroaching darkness. She funneled a fraction of the tiny flame against the shadow. It flickered and threatened to burn out, but she kept it fed from the center of her spirit, carrying it like a small candle toward the heart of the shadow.

The invader snarled and snapped. It raised a ruckus, flinging itself around to better distract her attention, but so long as the flame burned, it had no choice but to retreat.

Kaya's taste of success solidified her focus and taught her a truth about the shadow song she'd suspected but had never confirmed: in a fair fight, it was the weaker force, and it knew. So it didn't fight fair. It attacked hope and courage, convincing its victim there was no reason to resist. Only then could it gain ground and win.

She sat up straight in her chair and took a deep breath through her nose. This battle would be one of the longest of her life, so she made herself as comfortable as her bonds allowed. The war for her spirit was fought not in giant sweeping charges and retreats, but in the slow push of a boulder up a hill. Shadow gave her no chance to relax, no opportunity to regather her will and strength. Bit by bit, piece by piece, she fought the battle in the silence of her cell. Slowly, she regained what the shadow had taken.

The sound of footsteps approaching the door and another muttered conversation stole a precious slice of her focus. Shadow leaped into the gap, retaking in the beat of a heart what she'd spent much longer regaining.

The sudden loss coming from such a small mistake made her sag. Tears formed at the corners of her eyes, victory over the shadow as distant now as it had ever been. What was the point of fighting if defeat was never more than the blink of an eye away?

She ground her teeth tightly together and once again shoved the shadow out of her spirit. As before, shadow fought for every scrap of space, and she sensed it waiting for her to make another mistake, sensed it eager for a spirit like hers.

She wouldn't give it the pleasure.

Time stretched as Kaya fought the battle for her spirit. Without sunlight or food to mark the time, the battle could have lasted half a day or two and she wouldn't know the difference. Time meant nothing compared to the question of what fraction of her spirit was consumed by shadow.

She drove the shadow back to the very edges of her spirit, where it clung with the greatest tenacity she'd yet experienced. Her spirit had little strength left to it, and she could almost hear the whispers of shadow, seducing her into believing that a job mostly done was good enough, that she'd won already, and the last little bit didn't matter.

Kaya closed her spiritual ears to the shadow's plea, then gave one last shove. Its final claws ripped from her soul, and it was as if she'd pushed it off a cliff. It fled from her, and she was entirely Kaya once again. A tremor passed through her body as the Song reasserted its rightful place. Muscles tight from the strain of the battle relaxed, and Kaya once again slumped in her chair. She might have even slept for a time, but in the unchanging environment of her cell, she wasn't sure.

Freed from shadow, Kaya turned her attention to her next problem.

The reunion with her father had been unpleasant, and she'd rather not endure another. It was time to find her way out of here.

10

Radyn flew with four others on Tanwen's back, his old friend as capable of carrying all five as Radyn was a handful of potatoes. Physical strength and an ancient mastery of the Song kept him gliding across invisible currents of air with the ease of a sparrow in flight. Through their connection, Radyn experienced Tanwen's love of flight as though it were his own.

They'd shared the experience more times than Radyn could count, but with the new shards under his skin, the familiar sensations took on a vividness that threatened to overwhelm Radyn's tired mind. The boundary that separated him from the dragon was gossamer-thin, maintained more by Tanwen than by any effort on Radyn's part.

Radyn's wary gaze revealed not just the storm clouds ahead, but the shifting masses of air Tanwen would soon navigate, traced like ghostly wisps upon his vision. An updraft in front of the advancing storm flung them higher, eliciting a soft whoop of delight from one of the Daggers behind him.

His heart beat in a slow and steady tandem with Tanwen's, a beat he swore was echoed across the nearly two dozen dragons soaring toward the darkness. Radyn had never seen the entirety of Firestone's forces in the air at the same time, and it was an awesome sight. A single dragon loaded with riders was a fearsome force. This many warriors were enough to change the course of the world.

If Jyn felt any hesitation about committing or leading such a force, he gave no sign. He rode at the front of the clan, despite Magni's repeated attempts to convince him to assume a safer position somewhere near the center of the flight. He sat with his back straight, a conquering hero surveying his new territory.

The dragons gathered closer as they dropped altitude and approached the gray-veiled storm. They'd seen no sign of Nightkeep dragons in the sky, but they were in danger of losing one another once inside the storm. Lightning traced white-hot lines between the clouds, and it was the last light Radyn saw before he was enveloped by rain.

Radyn closed his eyes and pressed himself against Tanwen's neck. His meager human senses weren't capable in these conditions, but Tanwen's served them both. They flew close to the ground, the tops of the trees whipping beneath Tanwen's belly.

Jyn's dragon spread his wings and dropped into the clearing where they'd landed before. Three other dragons followed Jyn's lead, and the Daggers and Swords leaped from the dragons' backs with practiced efficiency. Tanwen and the other dragons circled close, alert for any dangers that approached through the trees and the bog.

The four dragons took off in unison, which allowed another four to drop into place as the first group of Manirah established a perimeter. Tanwen caught movement in the bog, which Radyn confirmed with his own eyes. Dark shapes darted from cover to cover, advancing upon the clearing. Several dragons roared, warning the warriors below of the danger.

The shadow warriors' reaction was no less than Jyn had planned for, but Radyn had held out hope their second arrival might surprise this mysterious enemy more than the first.

The second flight of dragons took off and a third landed. Manirah rushed to reinforce the perimeter as the dragons no longer carrying warriors hunted shadow warriors, and the scene below rapidly devolved into barely controlled chaos. The bog was thick with enemies swarming through the muck like ants guarding their hills. They knew the safe passages, the hidden trails that wouldn't suck their legs down to the knee in dark mud that refused to release its grip. Dragons prevented the shadow warriors from charging through the open spaces, allowing the Manirah time to organize a powerful defense.

Tanwen spread his wings as the fourth flight replaced the third in the clearing. Radyn's last observation before Tanwen's massive legs absorbed the gentle impact of the landing was that there had to be hundreds of enemies surrounding them, and for a brief moment, he worried he had argued Jyn into a battle that would strip Firestone of the last of its defenders.

Thinking ended as the Daggers behind him leaped off Tanwen's back. For most, it was their first foray into real battle, and their eagerness overwhelmed their caution. Radyn remained perched on Tanwen's neck for one moment more, letting his eyes roll over the battlefield one last time.

The perimeter was already well established, Swords and Daggers standing shoulder to shoulder as the first of the shadow warriors reached the line. Most of their enemies were armed only with steel, but a few among them carried dark blades. Firestone's dragons circled close to the perimeter, protecting the clan from archers and killing any of the warriors who dared cross an open space. Jyn's dragon bit down on one archer who had leaned out from the protection of a tree trunk, severing an arm and removing a chunk of flesh from the archer's shoulder.

Radyn dismounted Tanwen and encouraged him to take to the air once again. He hurried to the western edge of the clearing, where pre-selected Swords and Daggers gathered around him. The next flight of dragons landed, and their riders almost all joined Radyn. Soon after, the last flight of dragons took off from the clearing, leaving Radyn's assault force complete.

They formed a line three across, the point of their long spear headed by Radyn and a pair of senior Swords. Radyn's command sent them marching west, in the direction he'd last seen Kaya. Their movement didn't go unnoticed. Warriors originally destined for Jyn's perimeter scrambled through the mud and standing water, seeking trails that would allow them to cut Radyn's organized line into tattered ribbons.

Shadow warriors struck first near the tip of the spear, feet flying swiftly over the raised and packed trail. None carried steel, a sure sign of their quality. Radyn pulled the hilt free from his belt and connected to the shard within. The maniblade flicked to life in less than the blink of an eye, a pale blue light bright enough to illuminate half the battlefield. He met the first warrior, turning aside a wild swing and snapping his wrists, the maniblade cutting through flesh like paper.

The Swords beside him took only a moment longer to defeat the enemies that engaged them. The main force of enemies struck like a heavy wave crashing against a shore, bodies and blades pressed together in a fierce melee. Radyn's shards filled him with the Song, lifting his spirit above the ordinary din of battle, above the grunting and sweating, the curses and the blood. The quickest of the shadow warriors moved like a child struggling to hold a heavy sword for the first time. They fell before his maniblade, one cut blending into another as he carved his way toward Kaya.

Shouts behind him warned of trouble, but he didn't need to turn to sense the shape of it. Three warriors wide was all the narrow trail through the bog allowed, and it wasn't thick enough for the line to endure the vicious assault. Radyn and the senior Swords near the front of the line advanced, but the Daggers in the middle of the line fought tooth and nail against the strongest opponents they'd ever faced.

Most acquitted themselves well, but the enemy sensed the weakness in the line and pressed, throwing bodies at the Daggers until the line snapped in two, stranding Radyn, the senior Swords, and a handful of Daggers in a sea of shadow.

Radyn pressed his attack. Those left behind, if they were wise, would return to the perimeter Jyn had established, but he could spare them no further thought. He and the Swords broke through the last of the defenders, Radyn's maniblade opening a final opponent from hip to shoulder.

The trail they followed ended at a tree, and Radyn's advance came to a surprising end. "Search for wherever they hid her," he commanded. "It has to be close."

Swords and Daggers bent themselves to the task, and Radyn closed his eyes to interrogate senses that weren't entirely his own. The Song filled him and surrounded him, but his awareness stretched far beyond the limits of his hearing and sight.

Shadow thrived in this bog, thick and cold, but it had a heart, a darkness from which the web of shadow grew. It was below him, almost directly so. He followed the lines of force that extended from that beating heart of blackness and traced them, one at a time. Many stretched out beyond his awareness, and he let those go once he deemed them irrelevant to his cause.

One, though, rose into the tree before him, terminating in a complex web inscribed into the sturdy trunk. It reminded him, in a way, of the defenses the Singers had learned to weave around the Engine rooms, but if the web represented an entrance, Radyn had no ability to open it. He couldn't manipulate shadow any more than he could the path of a nuddu.

When all else failed, there was always brute force. He opened his eyes, the afterimage of the web a ghostly vision as he drew his maniblade back and thrust it deep into the heart of the web and the tree.

Maniblade bit deep into shadow and was stopped cold. Radyn gritted his teeth, connected with all his shards, and pushed deeper into the wood. He might as well have cut through a stone with a steel blade. "Help, please," he said through clenched teeth.

The senior Swords and Daggers returned from their fruitless hunt and joined Radyn. Their maniblades poked holes into the tree around the shadow net, making the thick bark look like an oversized pincushion. The assembled Manirah poured their spirits and the Song into the tree, and the shadow withered under the sustained light. The tree cracked open, splitting like dry wood beneath the blade of an ax, revealing an entrance.

Shadow warriors and Manirah alike turned at the

sound, and with a roar, the battle shifted toward the tree. Radyn glanced back and saw Magni stab an enemy through the back, but the enemy barely seemed to notice, so focused was he on protecting whatever the tree held.

The well-defined battle for the clearing spread into chaos as the warriors turned their full attention to Radyn's small force. The back half of Radyn's line was caught in the transition, a sudden barrier between those attacking the clan in the clearing and the newfound entrance.

Radyn's heart went out to the Manirah caught in the middle, but he turned his back on them and ran into the tree, into the darkness and shadow below.

THE WEB of tunnels and rooms lurking beneath the surface of the bog defied all reason, as though they personally delighted in confusing Radyn's sense of direction. The stairwell descended not into a bunker like Underhill, but a stretched-out series of curving hallways that rose and fell to no pattern or reason that he could discern. Polished stone reflected the dim light of flickering lanterns, powered not by the Song, nor by shadow, but by some energy beyond his understanding.

Fleeing footsteps echoed down empty hallways. Whether an evacuation or a gathering of forces, Radyn couldn't tell, but the irregular percussion reminded him that time grew short. He stretched out his senses and listened for Kaya's song, which sounded like a distant melody. No arcing passageway led straight toward her, and so Radyn pointed down a hallway that led in her general direction. The Swords and Daggers followed as they guarded against any attempts at flanking them.

The gentle bends, rises, and drops of the hallway soon

left Radyn lost and disoriented. The passages reminded him of the work of the Makers. These were hallways designed to endure, built with care to resist the relentless march of time and corrosion. Firestone's most talented architects couldn't do more than approximate the materials and techniques. Yet these passages couldn't have come from a Maker's mind. Radyn had never met them, but a lifetime living among their greatest works had given him a sense of his ancestors. Their minds had been ordered and logical, their designs favoring straight lines and right angles. These flowing hallways represented a similar level of achievement but a different mind, like a river that bent and curved to fit into the space given to it.

His sense of Kaya's position shifted, but so dizzying was the effect of the curving hallways, he wasn't sure if she had moved or if he and the other Manirah had run past her. He took the next turn that seemed appropriate and almost ran headfirst into a group of shadow warriors.

They were armed with nothing but steel, which likely explained why he hadn't sensed them. His maniblade flashed to life as he fell among them, their surprise as great as his. Those who survived his first pass were brought down by the senior Swords who followed a step behind, and then they were past, leaving little besides a spreading pool of blood on the polished stone.

Radyn swore as his sense of Kaya's position changed again. If laid end to end, these tunnels must stretch for miles, yet they were knotted together in a weave beyond comprehension. A short stretch of hallway connected two other passages that ran, at least for a moment, in parallel. He ducked down the connection, then reversed course down the parallel hallway.

She was getting closer, but who knew how much time they had before their ill-considered assault fell apart?

As if in response to his unspoken fear, a thought from Tanwen came into his mind. Radyn cursed out loud.

Their time was up.

Dragons from Nightkeep had been launched from above the storm clouds to join the battle below, and Radyn suspected they weren't coming to join his side.

11

Kaya sensed the change in the Song from her cell. What had once been a reasonably constant presence, like a tune being gently sung on the other side of a thick door, grew in volume and expanded in range. The change seeped through the cracks in the net of shadow that surrounded her room, dripped through the minuscule holes she'd made in the defenses. She drank deeply from the notes that trickled into her cell, the drops more refreshing than the water her captors refused to provide.

With refreshment came vigor, and she worried at the net around her cell with the additional strength. Pinpricks in the defense became full-fledged holes, and the trickle of the Song that snuck through became a drizzle. Her body and spirit lapped up the Song like a wolf at a clear stream after a long run.

The process iterated as her growing connection with the Song allowed her to attack the shadow with renewed strength, which in turn poured more strength into her spirit. As she carved deeper through the shadow, she sensed the spirits manipulating the Song in the world beyond her cell and smiled.

Far from being forgotten, Radyn and Jyn had come for her, and from her sense of the battle above, they'd brought almost every Manirah and dragon Firestone possessed.

Encouraged by her friends' willingness to sacrifice themselves on her behalf, her spirit focused the energies of the Song available to her and cut clean through the last webs of shadow that wrapped around the room. The remaining shadow, still connected to whatever source resided deep beneath the bog, retreated to safer territory. For the first time in what felt like ages, nothing stood between Kaya and the Song, and she welcomed it back into her weary spirit.

Strength refilled tired limbs and returned focus to a mind worn thin by her time in captivity. Imagination, will, and Song combined to form a sharp glowing dagger in her hand. She sliced through the bonds holding her in place. She stood and stretched as blood returned to limbs too long stationary, then turned her attention to the door and whatever lay beyond.

Kaya sensed neither Song nor shadow, but the door couldn't muffle completely the sound of two voices in conversation. She was unable to make out the words, but there was no doubt a heated debate was taking place.

The door was her only way out, but should she attempt to escape on her own or wait for rescue? Radyn should be able to sense her, for she could easily sense him now that the net of shadow had been cut, but there was no telling what resistance he faced. Given the size of the force they'd brought, she imagined it was considerable.

She listened once more at the door. The voices spoke softly, but they were close. She took a step back and extended the maniblade as far as she could. Without a hilt, it was about as long as a short sword. Better if it was longer, but it would have to do. Before she could question her choice, she ran the maniblade through the door and pulled hard across. It felt as though she struck something, but it could have been a door, flesh, or wall, and she wouldn't be sure of the difference. She cut around the lock and kicked the door open.

The door slammed into the second guard, a young lady dressed in flowing black robes who was stooping over the first guard, a young man wearing a similar style. His face had paled, though, and he slumped against the wall as he held his stomach as his body pumped blood through his slick fingers.

Kaya cut and cut again. Had Radyn been near to judge, he would have been disappointed. Her first slash cut through the young lady's spine, disabling her instantly, while her second missed the heart of the other. She cursed and twisted the blade, cutting up and toward the heart. He screamed in agony as her attempt at mercy turned into a final torture. His scream cut off as blood rushed up his throat and gagged him. His eyes darted left and right before he coughed up a large mug's worth of blood and went still.

The young lady was crying, trying to crawl away from Kaya because she couldn't get her legs to move. Tears sprang to Kaya's eyes.

"I'm sorry," she said, then drove the point of her blade into the young lady's skull, ending her misery.

A shudder passed through her, as though the shadow entwined with the halls of this cursed place drank up the offered blood and sought purchase in her spirit again. Weakened by the guilt of her actions, the shadow's grasp almost caught her. She clutched desperately to the Song, holding on to the maniblade as though it were all that kept her from drowning. The moment of weakness passed through her spirit and into her body, and she said a small thanks to the Song she hadn't been fed since she'd been captured, for she would have vomited any food they'd seen fit to offer her.

Once the bout of weakness passed, she shuffled down the hallway, which was like none she'd seen before. As capable as the Makers, perhaps, the halls bent and curved as though they were the veins of a living organism. She glanced back at the door she'd escaped from, but there was nothing that marked it as unique. It was a plain door in a hallway filled with plain doors. Hardly worth a thought, except for the two bodies sprawled across the floor.

Kaya stretched out her senses, seeking Radyn. He didn't seem far away, but the maze of hallways left her disoriented. Her first steps were hesitant, but before long she was hurrying, her feet slapping against the polished stone. The construction was more impressive than she would have assumed from the room she'd been locked in. No other warriors tried to stop her, but she sensed them rushing toward the source of the shadow. Questions of their purpose danced on the edge of her awareness, but reuniting with Radyn meant much more.

A figure, not much taller than her but certainly heavier, stepped into the hallway ahead. He stopped when he saw her. "Kaya?"

Her focus faltered as her father took three hesitant steps forward. Her thoughts froze as her body screamed at her to run, but it was as though the cords around her ankles had once again been tied to the floor.

"What are you doing out of your room?" he asked, like she was a child who'd snuck out in the middle of the night.

He stood between her and Radyn, and he no longer had any power over her. She moved to step around him.

Father raised his hand. "Stop!"

The note of command brought her to a stop, and an irrational fear seized her that he had some command over shadow, or over her body, she didn't yet understand. He smirked.

Her obedience turned out to be nothing more than fear icing her muscles into stillness. His unearned confidence stoked the flames of her anger, melting away the fear that locked her in place. The maniblade appeared in her hand as she stepped forward again, and his confidence fled like a startled deer before the shadow of a dragon. His eyes went wide, and she hated the intensity of the thrill that ran through her at the sight.

Firestone needed her.

If not for that, she might have remained, to inflict some fraction of the suffering back upon the man who'd been duty-bound by parentage to protect her. Shadows spread from the walls of the passage, embracing her, promising her the revenge she'd so long dreamed about. The pleasure that coursed through her at the thought horrified her, but she couldn't compel herself to look away.

"Kaya? What are you doing with that?"

She pointed the maniblade at his heart. "You were my father. You were the one supposed to protect me."

"I am your father, and I always have! I taught you, nurtured the power within you. Do you think you could have become what you are without me?"

Her answering smile was bitter, for he spoke a truth, though not the one he thought. She wouldn't have learned as she did if not for him, and despite everything, she was grateful, for because of him, she'd learned the Song like no one before her. At least, not since the time of the Makers. "You give yourself far too much credit."

The prick at his pride gave him the courage he

otherwise lacked. He stepped forward until the maniblade was almost cutting through his dark robes. "Put down the maniblade and return to your room. The Seer will teach you what I could not."

She shivered at the notes of adoration in his voice, but the tip of her weapon barely quivered. "My friends have come for me."

Father dismissed the fact with a wave of his hand. "And they were fools for doing so. They're locked in a battle on the surface with the Seer's allies, and now Nightkeep's dragons will fall upon them. They'll be crushed between two superior forces, and there will be nothing left. You saved them once before, but their gamble for your life will prove their final undoing."

She sensed no lie in his words, for he believed them with the same fervor he believed in his Seer. She pressed the tip of the maniblade into his flesh. "Then I shall perish with them."

Father snarled and raised his hand to slap her across the face. "Foolish girl!"

Tendrils of shadow song wrapped around her wrists, pulling her forward like a child eager to show her something, begging her to bury the maniblade in her father's chest. It promised an end to her worries, an absolute freedom she hadn't known since the day she was born.

Kaya snapped her wrist, slicing the tip of the maniblade across Father's chest, drawing a red line from the sternum and across his right breast. Blood spilled from the wound, only to be greedily consumed by his white robes. The maniblade sank deeper into his right arm as he tried to stop his swing. It cut cleanly through the muscles of his upper arm, which fell limp as they snapped.

Father screamed and lurched for her with his good left

arm. She ducked underneath and cut deep into the side of his leg, careful to miss the artery. His scream changed pitch as he tumbled down, landing like an oversized sack of meat. She didn't look back, afraid of her reaction if she did.

Her heart pounded in her chest, torn in several directions at once. He was the creator of most of her misery and a pathetic excuse for a parent. He served the shadow song and its terrible logic. But he was still Father, and if she followed her memories back far enough, there was warmth and light between them. He'd loved her like he should have, once, and a part of her that had never fully matured hoped that one day he would again.

Cold reason argued for his death, for the elimination not just of her enemy, but for an enemy of all humanity. But to serve that judgment meant surrendering the last sliver of hope that redemption awaited him, and she couldn't. Not if she wanted to live with herself after.

Her attempt to walk away was arrested by his cry, high-pitched like a child in distress calling for his parents. "What did you do to me?"

The pain and confusion in the question ripped her certainty to shreds, and she almost turned. Instead, she let the maniblade vanish as she took in a deep, shuddering breath. She held tight to the Song and let its gentle warmth burn the shadow away. Father's actions didn't deserve mercy, but his spirit needed it all the same.

When she felt her spirit centered and steady, she turned back to him. He lay in a heap, a small pool of blood collecting beneath him. He looked like an oversized injured child, his face pale and lined with confusion. Her spirit cracked at the sight, but the Song held it together. Who knew what effect the prolonged exposure to shadow had on him? Her own battle with the shadow song had taught her that it didn't transform, it simply unmasked. Beneath the mantle of his authority as a Singer, Father had always been lost and uncertain, given all the power in the world but without the values needed to guide that strength. He'd risen to a position of nearly ultimate authority, only to realize that what he desired most was to have someone tell him what to do. In answer to his unspoken plea, the shadow song offered him the Seer and his cult.

For a moment, she'd broken shadow's iron grip on his spirit. Perhaps in that confusion, she could plant a seed that would otherwise find his spirit too hostile to take root in. She didn't dare step within his reach, but she turned away from her own need to escape to squat near him. "I'm sorry, Father, but I believe the Song is good, and that humanity is one of its most cherished instruments. We are flawed and weak, but I've been blessed to see the strength within so many spirits. I haven't given up on humanity, just as I haven't given up on you."

Father was silent as he stared at her, and she swore the words wormed their way into his spirit. Then the openness in his gaze closed, and his expression was flat, hard, and angry. "You cut me!"

Kaya stood. Shadow had closed its grip on him again, and nothing she said now would matter. She could only hope that her words had reached him, and that they'd managed to find somewhere to root before darkness once again overshadowed his spirit.

It cut at her own spirit to turn away, even though she knew it was right.

He shouted at her and cursed her name as she turned the corner and left him behind.

12

R adyn took two more turns before they ran into Kaya. The strength of her spirit almost blinded his senses, brighter than he'd ever sensed her before. He wrapped her in a tight embrace, then held on to her shoulders as he took a step back and examined her.

The skin around her ankles and wrists was raw, cut, and bleeding. She'd lost weight in the short time they'd been separated, and the gash on her head looked dirty and angry. She smelled of dried sweat, mud, and grime. Despite the rough treatment she'd clearly endured, she was on her feet and her eyes practically shone in the dim hallways.

"I came to rescue you, but it seems you've already taken care of the hard part without me," he said.

She smiled at his attempt at humor, though her exhaustion meant the smile couldn't quite reach her eyes. "It's still good to see you."

"You, too. Can you run and fight?"

"Maybe not fight, but I can run."

"Good enough. Let's go."

He nodded to one of the senior Swords, who led the way back through the maze. They'd taken to carving small arrows in the walls with their maniblades, leaving them a trail to follow out. One Sword led, the other remained to act as the rearguard, and Radyn and the two Daggers stuck close to Kaya.

Their escape through the twisting hallways remained unopposed, but they moved too quickly for Radyn to question their good fortune. They returned to the broken stairwell in far less time than they'd needed to find Kaya. The shouts of warriors above mingled with the cries of the wounded and injured. Radyn held them from the stairs for one moment to give them a chance to breathe and prepare for the battle.

He also gave them one final order. "Whatever happens, get Kaya back to Tanwen. You don't need to reach the clearing. Just find someplace he can swoop in."

When he was sure his words had been heard, he nodded and led the way up the stairs and into the maelstrom of shadow and Song. The number of shadow warriors had only grown since Radyn had disappeared into the tunnels below, and Firestone's clan was pressed hard. Jyn and Magni held the perimeter of the clearing, blazing like twin suns offering the world the last of their heat. A small knot of Manirah held the entrance to the tunnels, but there were more bodies cooling on the ground than fighting.

Radyn connected with all the shards in his body and leaped into the battle, a single man with dreams of becoming a shield wall. His maniblade flashed between the raindrops, cleaving any who attempted to defend.

The violence of his attack gave the knot of Manirah a precious moment to set their feet, take a deep breath, and push deeper into the mass of shadow warriors. The senior

Swords that had followed Radyn into the tunnels fell back to guard Kaya, who immediately attracted the ire of several dark-robed warriors.

Radyn's advance stalled as a tall, dark-haired warrior thin enough to be made of wire challenged him. In a contest of pure strength, Radyn would have triumphed without question, but the man carried a dark sword that flickered with impossible speed. Radyn parried and let the shadow slide off his maniblade, then drove his shoulder at the man.

Only to strike empty air as the man twisted away, snapping his sword at Radyn's back. Radyn twisted and formed a maniblade in his off hand without a hilt, catching the deadly shadow and stopping it cold. He planted his foot and chopped wildly at the man with hilt and maniblade.

The wiry enemy drifted back, stepping over a fallen comrade as he walked backward. Radyn pursued, but other warriors, eager to contribute to Radyn's downfall, swarmed him with shadow and steel. Radyn surrendered the steps he'd gained, his momentum spent. It became all he could do to stay ahead of the weapons hungry for a sliver of flesh.

One step back became another, followed soon by another, and it wouldn't be long before he would be choosing the place he fell.

A dragon dropped from the sky, cracking ancient trees like twigs as it crushed dozens of enemies beneath its bulk. Radyn stumbled and almost slipped in the blood and mud as the ground shook beneath him.

Radyn recognized Jyn's dragon. It clawed and twisted, whipped its tail as it snapped its jaw at any black-clad enemy. Its arrival cast the enemy ranks into chaos. Bodies flew through the air and broke against trees as the dragon's inhuman strength cleared the battlefield.

Radyn lashed out as shadow warriors turned to address the new enemy, once again closing the gap between him and Jyn. Torn between maniblade and claw, the shadow warriors fell like wheat before the scythe.

Jyn's dragon spread its wings and flexed its legs. The Song gathered its power as it prepared to take to the sky.

Dark swords, led by the wiry man who'd halted Radyn's advance, reached the dragon as it turned its attention to the sky. They plunged into the dragon wherever they could find unarmored flesh. Swords were buried in its stomach, legs, and neck. Blood poured from the wounds as the dragon roared, a cry of agony that almost brought Radyn to his knees, his spirit breaking as the dragon's body died.

He wasn't the only one affected. All the Manirah, attuned to the Song which the dragons served, stumbled back, pale and weak. The final cry of the dragon was as though a ghost had reached into Radyn's spirit and clutched it tight in an icy grip.

It was easy, at times, to forget the overwhelming power of a dragon. Their alliance with Manirah was mutually beneficial, but it was the Manirah's intelligence and foresight which they most contributed to the relationship. That made it too easy to feel superior, to believe that despite the dragon's size, their mastery of the Song, and their ability to fly, humans were somehow more.

Jyn's dragon was no ordinary dragon, though. It was an elder, an ancient who had watched the Makers before they had fled the surface for the skies. A creature that had lived in harmony with the Song for more years than a child could imagine.

The dragon's death reminded Radyn how wrong he

was. He'd sensed souls pass to the Gate before, but never had he heard the Song respond. It vibrated in his spirit, a discordant wail of mourning for one of the greatest of its servants. Even their enemies, enraptured by shadow, were still connected to the Song, their lives inexplicably entwined, and they, too, suffered as the Dragon breathed its last.

The battle ground to a halt as the combatant's souls labored under the sudden burden of grief. Radyn wanted nothing more than to lie down and wail, sorry for any crime he'd ever committed against the Song.

Compelled as he was, the effect struck their enemies worse. They clutched at their heads and at their chests, their eyes wide with abject terror.

Radyn forced Kaya to her feet and ordered the Manirah to follow him. They danced between the flailing forms of their enemies and around the fallen dragon. Mud sucked at their boots, but with a desperate effort, Radyn and the others reunited with Jyn.

The Blade looked as though someone had reached into his chest and scooped out his soul. His grip on his maniblade was loose, and he swayed on his feet as though the victim of a disorienting punch. Tears collected in the corners of his eyes, but he held his head high, preventing them from falling. Radyn went straight to him. "We should go before we can't."

Jyn's eyes were as cold as ice when they swiveled down to meet Radyn's gaze. "They deserve to die."

Already the first of the black-robed warriors were beginning to rise to their feet and shake off the grief that had stricken their hearts. Radyn shook his head. "I don't disagree, but now is not the time. They'll overwhelm us if we stay."

Jyn's spirit burned against Radyn's senses so powerfully Radyn took a step back. "No, they won't."

"Jyn! I'm sorry, but we've found what we came for. I'm leaving with Kaya. Firestone needs us."

He called to Tanwen, who was close. The sorrow that reverberated through their connection stole the breath from Radyn, but he bore some small fraction of his friend's grief and carried it as his own. The dragon dropped into the clearing.

Kaya grabbed Radyn's wrist. "Nightkeep's dragons are still descending through the storm, right?"

He nodded.

"Then let me connect with Tanwen."

Every fiber of his being argued against the idea, for it meant he would be taking to the sky without any defense, without any weapon that he could use to fight for and protect her. He searched her spirit and found no nervousness or uncertainty.

Such was his trust in her that he simply nodded again. He'd put his life in her hands before, and would do so again without hesitation or regret.

Truthfully, against the force that descended against them, there was nothing he could do. If they had any hope, it was in the connection she had developed with the Song.

Their choice agreed, she climbed onto Tanwen's back and waited for the others to follow. Then she asked Tanwen to launch them heavenward, away from the massacre happening in the mud and toward the one awaiting them in the clouds.

13

Kaya's heart, already battered and bruised by the successive encounters with the Seer, the shadow song, and her father, wept anew at the death of the elder dragon. The majestic creatures had never been gifted immortality, but the span of their lives was such that they seemed as such to those fortunate enough to spend time around them. The loss of so much wisdom was a terrible blow already, but the mourning notes of the Song of the Engines revealed a depth of grief beyond what Kaya had known was possible. Every spirit fighting on that battlefield felt as though they'd lost a wife, a husband, or a child.

It was all Kaya could do to follow Radyn as he pulled her toward the clearing. How he fought through the grief she didn't understand, but his firm grip on her wrist never faltered. She pulled her strength from him and centered her unsteady spirit.

The dragon's sacrifice gave them the space to escape the bog, but it meant little with the dragons from Nightkeep descending. Without a connection to Tanwen, she couldn't guess how many were on the way, but she assumed the number was high. Now that Nightkeep was stirred to action, they'd move decisively, and they had the dragons and riders to wipe Firestone's surviving force from the sky.

If it came to a fight, the result was inevitable.

As Radyn and Jyn argued, she searched for another path, and it didn't take her too long to find one. The idea chilled her to the bone, and so she continued to pursue other alternatives, but none came to mind.

She'd long ago promised herself there were things she wouldn't do, flexes of her strength she would always avoid. It wasn't just that the consequences were unpredictable, true though that would be. It was that, in so doing, she walked a path incredibly close to the one shadow had once wanted her to walk. Scholars could argue until they were blue in the face whether an evil act done out of noble intent was somehow different or better than one done out of malice, but none of it mattered when she was the one contemplating the act.

Violence was violence, and to be avoided, regardless of the cause. The paradox was that it was violence that shielded them from the unrestrained advance of shadow.

She hadn't thought it was possible for her heart to grow heavier after the death of the dragon, but life had a way of reminding her such absolutes were never as solid as she wanted them to be. She searched one last time for another path, but when none appeared, she asked Radyn for Tanwen, and being the trusting spirit he was, he agreed without question. He dropped his connection instantly, allowing her to seek out and join with Tanwen's spirit.

She'd guessed correctly the size of Nightkeep's force, and her commitment to her plan deepened. No other way existed.

They took to the air, the wind and rain lashing against

her face a welcome relief from her cell and the mud of the battleground. Nature wiped her clean of the events below, and she directed Tanwen away from the descending Nightkeep dragons. They were already too close.

As she'd hoped, several of the dragons in the lead shifted their course to pursue Tanwen, giving Firestone's Manirah precious extra moments to climb upon the other dragons and flee the battle. Even Jyn, broken by grief, climbed upon the last of the fleeing dragons. She breathed a deep sigh of relief as Firestone's allies took to the air.

With one battle behind, she turned her full attention to the dangers above. The descending dragons had the advantage of the higher altitude, which they could sacrifice for greater speed if they chose. Her time grew short.

"Give them a merry chase," she told Tanwen, who gave her a curt acknowledgement. The dragon cloaked itself with the Song and surged forward, forcing their pursuers to do the same.

Kaya had little choice but to entrust their flight to Tanwen, for her attention was needed elsewhere. She gripped his scales firmly and pressed herself tight against his neck, squeezing with her thighs for extra stability. Then she closed her eyes and dropped into the Song.

The music welcomed her with open arms, even as it mourned the loss of the elder dragon. With her physical body sandwiched between Radyn and Tanwen, the Song was nearly as loud and clear as when she sat beside Underhill's Engine. She let the Song embrace her and move through her as she let her spirit soak up the harmonies of a deeper reality.

She caught familiar phrases and movements, for despite the loss of a friend and the struggle for survival happening in her vicinity, life went on as it always had in the other corners of the world. Animals hunted for food and fled predators while plants reached for the sun, tracing its path against the sky with their petals.

In this, at least, the Seer had glanced a part of Truth. This world's life would survive beyond the extinction of humanity. What he missed, though, was how closely the notes of the Song followed humanity's achievements and failures. Singers didn't just manipulate the Song. They joined their voices with its notes, and though their efforts were painfully crude, there was a beauty in the effort, the same as when a child's untrained voice tried to harmonize with a mother's practiced melody.

Kaya spared a moment to soak the Song into her spirit, for what she was about to attempt couldn't be completed as a command. The working was too great, even for her. Alone, she was nothing against the might of an Engine. No Singer was.

Had Radyn asked her what she did, she couldn't explain. Her techniques weren't based on the logical and ordered curriculum the Singers drilled into their students. They were derived from pure awareness and intuition, of instincts honed by listening day after day, her spirit constantly attuned to the slightest of changes in the Song.

She sought Nightkeep's three mighty Engines, which posed no trouble at all. They were the Engines of her childhood, her first true friends, and she knew their Song almost as well as she now knew Underhill's. Her spirit danced to their tune, still healthy and strong despite the decay shadow had triggered. If the future was unchanged, Nightkeep wouldn't fly forever, but it would last much longer than any other city.

Their Song shifted as her spirit neared, a change she interpreted as joy and welcome. Nightkeep had never been home, but these Engines had been. They'd taught her so much of what she now knew. She danced and humbled her spirit before them, then listened closely to their notes and the silences between, familiarizing herself once again with the Engines.

There.

It wasn't as obvious as a drum beating out the rhythm of a piece of music, but there was a pattern to the Song. A heartbeat, perhaps. She chose one of the smaller Engines and came closer, thankful the Singers hadn't noticed her yet. But they wouldn't. To them, her spirit was just one quiet note among the much stronger background of the Engines.

She wrapped her spirit around her chosen Engine. Her heartbeat matched its own, and she lifted her voice to match its.

Her sense of self dissolved as her spirit beat in time and sang with the Engine. Like two lovers closely entwined on the dance floor, it was hard to tell where her spirit ended and the Song began. The Engine accepted her as its partner, though, and when she slowed the beat of its Song, it obeyed. Certain she was capable, she held her breath and held the silence between the beats for a count of two.

She'd listened to Radyn describe the story of what Firestone now called "The Little Fall," and his vivid retellings had always chilled her to the bone. Despite the fact they lived in what were essentially flying mountains, most people found it easy to forget they lived high above a surface that no longer welcomed them. The decking beneath their feet was as unmoving as the stone they built their apartments in.

She'd never imagined she would be the one to cause such a fall.

Wrapped up in the Song of the Engine, it was as nothing to her, a brief rest between two measures of music, and then the Engine resumed the duties it had faithfully fulfilled for so many generations. The Song continued, uninterrupted, but within moments it was joined by the discordant and unsettled voices of the Singers. They searched for the cause, and for her plan to work, they needed to find it.

Kaya borrowed some of the strength from the Engine and let her spirit burn so bright the other Singers couldn't help but notice her. Not only that, but they couldn't help but notice that she had their Engine under her complete control. As expected, their counterattack came quickly as they attempted to pull her spirit away from the Engine.

They'd have had better luck trying to persuade Radyn to voluntarily give up Elora's maniblade. She and the Engine were intertwined, and there were none that came close to possessing the skill necessary to do anything about it.

She held the silence between beats for a count of one, hoping her unspoken message would be clearly heard. The Singers cried out as their home dropped beneath their feet.

She didn't allow herself to imagine the plight of Nightkeep's citizens, most of whom she assumed were innocent of the actions of its Manirah and Singers. To do so would break her from the deep trance of unity she embraced. The only hope she spared was that the Singers wouldn't force her to follow through on her threat.

She didn't want to learn what she was capable of. Didn't want to learn how far she'd go to protect herself.

She sensed the retreat through her continued connection with Tanwen. The Nightkeep dragons descending upon them spread their wings wide, banked away, and began the long climb back to Nightkeep's position above the storm clouds. Kaya continued her dance with the Nightkeep Engine until she was sure the dragons wouldn't return. Then she stepped away, bowed toward her partner, and reunited the distant fragments of her spirit with her body.

Physical sensation once again took precedence, and she felt Tanwen's rough scales between her thighs and Radyn's congratulatory hand on her shoulder as the last of the rain whipped past her head. Tanwen's speed sent them clear of the storm in short order, and the warmth of sun on Kaya's skin was more than welcome, an old friend she hadn't fully realized how much she missed.

The Song rang brightly within her, and she didn't mind. She never wanted to be cut off from it again.

She asked Tanwen to take her home, and the dragon was more than happy to comply.

<h1 style="text-align:center">14</h1>

The Seer strode across the remains of the battlefield, though he had no interest in the bodies of either the Manirah or his allies from the surface. He made instead for the corpse of the dragon, which was the center of attention after its death as much as it had been during its life.

Dark-robed figures swarmed around the corpse like an army of overactive ants. Spears dug into unresisting flesh, prying off its armored hide one scale at a time. Daggers carved flesh from the enormous beast. Bloody grins told the Seer that not all the carved meat would make it to the fires already burning throughout the bog. None that he passed seemed upset that he had lost the girl, nor did he suffer any silent accusations surrounding the deaths of so many. Though Firestone's cost to rescue Kaya had been steep, it was only a fraction of what his allies had suffered.

No surprise, that. Though he despised the Manirah, he respected their strength, and the average Dagger was stronger than any of his allies who carried mere steel. It was of no concern to him, though. His allies were more numerous than anyone in the cities guessed, even now, and the well of hate they drew upon was deep. Those in the cities couldn't imagine how many enemies they possessed, nor how driven they were to bring the cities down.

In this, the dark-robed warriors were the perfect allies for his life's task, carefully groomed over generations to serve his master's bidding.

So though he turned his nose up at the sight of the dragon being slaughtered with less respect than a cow, it never occurred to him to put a stop to it. To the shadow warriors, the dragons were a sign of oppression, of a promise made with the cities that had never extended to them. They served only to deepen the grudges between ground and sky, a reminder that the cities that had already escaped the massacres of the past were also given the gift of the skies while those that fought on the surface scrambled in the mud to survive.

There was a shout of triumph from near the dragon's head, and the Seer's stomach churned as he watched a pair of warriors pull the dragon's golden eye free from its socket. It fell out with a sickening pull of liquid and dangled from nerves that were as thick as heavy rope. The Seer turned away before he grew sick. He'd seen enough.

He reached the firm path through the bog that led to the shrine, his boots sinking into the blood-infused soil. The noise and the activity quieted as he approached. They celebrated the dragon's death, but mourned the damage to their shrine, a gift from some of their earliest ancestors.

He stared at the destruction and shook his head, his master's ways still a mystery. He worked his way through the warriors, examining the damage. Belzrak was among them, and he had a hard stare for the Seer as he passed into the passages below. The undulating hallways kept no secrets from him. Shadow told him where he would find his wounded ally. He knocked on the door before opening it.

Presnell sat up at his arrival, though the motion agonized him. The wound across his chest was little more than a scratch, but the healing powers of the surface-dwellers hadn't been strong enough to fully heal the cut through his arm. By the time they returned to Nightkeep, it was anyone's guess if the healers would be able to return the right arm to use.

Presnell bowed. "Master."

The Seer feigned concern. Strange, that Presnell should help him seek to end all human life but still require the warmth and comfort of friendship. All humans were hypocrites, but in some the hypocrisy went far deeper than others. "It is good to see you up and about, old friend."

"Thank you, Master. I apologize again for allowing my daughter to escape."

Like he could have done anything. If his daughter hadn't cut him down, Radyn and the Swords wandering the halls would have. Presnell had his uses, but combat wasn't anywhere near that short list. "She caught us all by surprise," he said.

That was a truth. The commands from his master had been unmistakeable, and their purpose clear enough. Kaya was to convert, either by force or persuasion. The gift of shadow he'd blessed her with before he left should have been more than enough. His master had been satisfied as he'd taken leave of the room.

Presnell's eyes were unfocused. Belzrak's healers had given him some of their herbs to numb the pain of healing, and the effect hadn't yet fully worn off. "She did, didn't she. A remarkable woman she's become. Born of my seed and trained under a program of my own devising. The fools will have to listen to me now."

The Nightkeep Singer had his eyes at the Seer's feet, so he didn't see the Seer scowl. Presnell was a pathetic creature, so desperate to be seen as great by his peers, but so unwilling to put in the work that might have actually made him so. He was tremendously gifted with the Song, and it was no wonder his daughter was, too, but he'd always assumed his natural talent would be enough.

Presnell continued, maybe not even aware the Seer stood before him anymore. "When she comes to understand the truth, no one will stand against us." He straightened, his spine stiffening. "But what she needs is discipline. A firm hand. It's not right for a child to raise their hand against their father. Yes, she needs discipline, and I shall be the one to give it to her."

Presnell looked up and startled, as though noticing the Seer for the first time. Shadows of doubt crossed his face. So eager was he to be a part of something that mattered, he'd been an easy convert. But that eagerness made him sensitive to worries. Whenever something didn't go their way, he questioned it all. "Master, how did she escape? You told me that shadow had her firmly in its grip."

"The shadow's vision is deep, my old friend. You spoke with her, you noted her resistance to your kindness and generosity. When I visited her, I unveiled the truth for the very first time. I, too, had hoped she would convert the moment she learned the truth, but shadow knows better. It knows a seed has been planted in your daughter, but that seed needs time to bloom into the flower of devotion I know it will someday become."

Presnell nodded, eyes brightening as his weak spirit was reassured. "I'm glad, Master. I'm sorry that I doubted."

"There is nothing to apologize for. Shadow is in control, but faith is sometimes hard. Get some rest, for I'm sure we'll be summoned to Nightkeep soon."

If there was any meeting he dreaded more than this one, it would be that inevitable confrontation. He'd promised much to Nightkeep to gain their alliance, and so far, he'd only delivered on a few of his promises.

He left Presnell to whatever thoughts ran through the Singer's mind while he was alone, then made his way deeper into the ruins, toward the room where they kept the shrine. Two of Belzrak's guards stood outside the door, but they let the Seer in without fuss.

Belzrak's fear of the shrine had decreased in the days they'd been here, but he still stopped five full paces away and was unwilling to get closer. He'd brought in a cushion to kneel on while he contemplated the cube. Without turning, he said, "Events did not go as you foresaw."

A not-so-subtle dig at the title given to him by his sky-born followers, but the Seer let the comment slide off. The scavengers who called the mud of this world home respected strength above all else, and would have little respect for anyone who cried about being called names.

"I am no more than a servant of the shadow song, the same as you."

Belzrak thought on this claim for longer than the Seer expected, then shook his head slowly, as though he'd reached a weighty conclusion. "Not the same as us, I think."

The Seer said nothing, allowing the chief of this clan the opportunity to make his argument. "We listen to the shadow song, the same as you, but our skills have never advanced past the blades we wield. Your gift is something different, something greater. The shadow song has blessed you in ways we haven't seen before. You are a powerful man, but still a man. Today should not have happened."

"Your warriors brought down an elder dragon. Many of Firestone's warriors are dead."

Belzrak waved the argument away. "And my warriors will celebrate what they've achieved, but their hatred blinds them to the dangers. The girl understands the power of the shrine. If not now, then certainly later, when the nuddu crush her home. They will return then, and in numbers we cannot defend against."

"The shrine must be protected," the Seer agreed.

"We will take it back to our homelands. The sky clans won't seek it then."

The shadow song vibrated, a high note that caused both the Seer and Belzrak to wince. Belzrak's head snapped around to face the Seer. "What did it say?"

"You are right. It believes the Manirah will come for it, and that it belongs someplace safer."

Belzrak nodded, deeply satisfied the shadow song agreed.

The Seer imagined the shrine's long journey south toward the equator, the homelands of Belzrak's clan. The quest would take weeks, at the least. More than enough time for Kaya and the others to attack. "May I offer a suggestion you won't like?"

Belzrak tensed, but allowed him to continue.

"Bring it up to Nightkeep for safekeeping and transport. If Firestone and its allies are tempted to attack, it will be safer there than here on the surface."

Belzrak was on his feet in a second. "Our shrine will never bless one of those cursed cities!"

The Seer met Belzrak's glare. "Think! You've said yourself you cannot protect it if Firestone comes in force, and especially not if they have allies. Nightkeep can bring it to your homelands faster, and none of the cities would dare attack us. Nor will they have the time, once they realize the danger they're in. You may not like it, but it's the safest way to move the shrine. It's the only way we keep it safe."

Belzrak snarled and said something in his native language, which the Seer was certain was a curse. He paced the room for a few moments, never getting closer to the shrine than he was already. "I will want many of my warriors guarding it."

A reasonable request, and one the Seer was happy to bargain for. On average, he found the land-based clan members more amenable to all his requests. They understood his strength even better than those who followed him from the cities. "Of course. I'll ask for as many as Nightkeep will allow."

Belzrak had other demands, all of which the Seer agreed to fight for. The conversation only took a sliver of his attention, though, for shadow's plan began to reveal itself to him.

The moment had come.

It was time for the shrines to come together.

15

Radyn's return to Underhill left a lingering bitterness in the back of his throat. Those that survived were welcomed with open arms and tears of relief, but the cost of recovering Kaya had been steep. Husband, wives, and children had gathered outside the main entrance as the dragons came in for the landing, hopeful gazes searching for familiar outlines and gaits. Far too many were left wanting.

The responsibility for their loss ultimately fell to Jyn, for the Blade commanded the Manirah of Firestone, and he wasn't one to share that burden, no matter how the responsibility should rightfully be spread. Wracked by a deeply personal sorrow for the loss of the elder dragon, Jyn confronted those hopeful faces and broke the sad news of their grief. Radyn approached the knot of civilians that had gathered to hear the Blade speak, thinking he might help the Blade bear some of the burden, but a sharp gesture from Magni diverted his intent.

He stood for a moment, alone, then turned toward the main gates. Aria hadn't come to greet him, and he suspected it was because she was resting in their apartment. Growing a child was no easy feat, and her need for rest had increased in the past month. Radyn wished she would reduce her other efforts, but rarely spoke his mind. Convincing Aria to do less was a battle he would never win.

Once past the commotion of the main gates, Underhill's hallways were quiet, as though he walked them in the middle of night instead of late afternoon. The emptiness suited his mood, and his steps were slow as he unconsciously followed the oft-trodden path toward his apartment. Jyn would no doubt be meeting with his commanders and Kaya soon, but there was a little time. The threat of the nuddu, which grew by the moment, seemed somehow distant. Radyn couldn't summon the strength to care, though he knew he should.

The door to their apartment opened on silent hinges and Radyn slipped through as quiet as a ghost. He pulled off his boots and padded across the floor to their bedroom, where Aria was fast asleep, snoring lightly. Radyn smiled at the sight, then went to the washroom, where he stripped out of his filthy clothes and hopped into the shower. The shower was, as always, short, but he stepped out with skin rubbed raw.

He dried himself off and then walked naked back into the apartment, breathing in the silence and exhaling the invisible weight that hung from his shoulders. He looked down at his hands and picked at a fleck of dried blood he'd somehow missed in the shower. It fought his efforts for longer than it should have, and he swore as he redoubled his effort. Finally, the blood lost its grip, and he rubbed the spot with his thumb, ensuring it was clean.

Radyn stared at his hands, now more calloused from wielding hoes, pitchforks, and spades than maniblades. He breathed out long and slow again. Far easier to clean dirt and mud off his hands than blood.

Far easier.

He inspected himself one last time, then snuck into the bedroom and gently lay down next to Aria. She stirred at his arrival, shifting so her side was pressed against his. He worked his arm under her head and she nuzzled into his shoulder. Her right arm sought his, pulling it over until it was resting on her stomach.

Their child kicked his hand.

"He's as strong as his mother," Radyn said.

Aria smiled. "Did you bring her back?"

"I did. It cost us dearly, though."

She snuggled closer, and if it had been in Radyn's power, he would have spent the rest of his days frozen just like this. She'd heard the hurt in his voice, for she said, "If not for them, it would have been all of us."

There was no arguing with the obvious. "I know. Doesn't stop me from wishing that we didn't have to fight and kill just to survive." He pressed his hand more firmly against her stomach. "I want him to grow up in a world where he has better choices."

Aria's eyes opened, fully awake now. "It's what I want, too. Unfortunately, though, you're going to have to fight to make that world come true."

"I know."

They lay in bed in silence, and Radyn's thoughts wandered aimlessly for a time.

Finally, he said, "With every year that passes, I think I understand my father a bit better. When I was young, I could never figure out why he put away his maniblade and became a farmer. Now the decision seems like the very definition of wisdom."

"He did well in raising you in the time that he had. Just like you'll do well with our son."

It wasn't so much the words, but the certainty with which she uttered them, that rekindled the dwindling fire in Radyn's spirit. He held her close for a few moments longer, then began the slow process of untangling himself. "Thank you."

She stretched languorously on the bed, and it was all Radyn could do not to jump back in beside her. "You're a cruel temptress," he said.

She grinned wide. "Just need to remind you there's an excellent reason for you to hurry back."

He threw on a fresh set of clothes and bent down and kissed her stomach. "More than one."

KAYA HAD little need for the gathering upon her return. Radyn had slipped away into the quiet halls of Underhill, and Kaya's spirit pulled that direction, too. Orenil stood among a group of Singers that had come out to greet the new arrivals, and he had his eyes fixed on her, but she wasn't ready to go to him, not yet.

She ducked into the crowd, grateful for once that she wasn't too tall. She walked between families reuniting and partners squeezing their way toward Jyn. A nervous energy ran through the crowd, and for good reason. The nuddu were still on their way. Given their pace and location, probably not more than a day away, or maybe a little more.

It would fall to Jyn to offer reassurance, and Kaya said a silent thanks the responsibility wasn't hers. Her gifts required truth, and she didn't think she could bend it enough to offer the gathered citizens what they needed.

Especially not now.

She crept from group to group until she passed through the main gate unobserved.

Underhill's Engine's Song was sweet and welcoming, and Kaya took turn after turn that led toward the sealed chamber. Eventually, she came to a thick steel door guarded by two Manirah and a panel.

The change saddened her. When she'd first arrived at Underhill, the Engine had been on the brink of death. She'd nursed it back to life, reinvigorated it with her Song. Because hardly any people knew where the soulkeeper ruins were, and because they simply didn't have the people or need to guard it, the Engine room had been open to all. Children had wandered through as she sang, their eager and innocent questions always welcome, even though it slowed her work.

It had been such a change from her earlier childhood at Nightkeep, in which access to the Engines had been closely guarded. It was all for good reason, of course, and as much as she despised most of Nightkeep's methods, she couldn't quite bring herself to fault them for protecting their Engines as they did. The problem was that it turned the Engines from something natural and wonderful into something sacred and mythical. Most citizens never saw an Engine their entire lives, never once experienced firsthand the power of the stones that kept them all alive. Even the Swords and Daggers only saw it on rare occasion, never more than once or twice in their entire lives.

Underhill's approach, by necessity, had been different, and most of the original children had grown up with the Engine as a normal part of their lives. Kaya hoped that as they developed a sensitivity to the Song, it would make them more likely to become a Singer who followed in her footsteps, rather than the rigid and proscribed paths the clan Singers followed.

But of course, she understood the necessity. It had been made clear the last time Underhill had come under attack. The Engine now kept them alive, and there were forces that sought to destroy it. The nuddu were pretty clear evidence of that.

The Swords bowed to her and welcomed her back, and she thanked them as she pressed her palm to the pillar Aria had originally designed for Firestone. One of Jyn's first pointed suggestions had been a set of security measures similar to what Firestone's Engine had enjoyed, and Miranda had been more than happy to agree.

She sang, and the pillar recognized her and opened the door. With a final bow to the guards, she stepped beyond the door and made sure it sealed shut behind her. Then it was onward to the Engine room. The familiar pale blue glow welcomed her, and she found a little alcove that would be quiet, even if other Singers came in.

She pressed herself into the alcove so she wouldn't be seen, curling her legs up tight against her chest as she stared at Underhill's Engine. She didn't dare sing to it, didn't dare open herself up to the power of the Song, not now. Like the citizens outside the main gates, she sought comfort. The Engine and its Song had provided it before, but perhaps it was foolish to ask comfort from the Song now.

Her whole body trembled and shivered.

She should have gone to Radyn and Aria and stolen a bit of the warmth that seemed to effortlessly flow between them. They would have offered it to her without question, but she wasn't ready to burden them with her suspicions. Not yet.

The Song was still alive in her.

It was alive in them all, whether people acknowledged it or not, for it was intertwined with life itself, but not like it was with her. Not like it was right now.

She'd been a fool. A fool and more. Too proud and too certain of her abilities.

She'd danced with the Engines, sang like she never had before. In the midst of it all, and driven by desperation and need, she'd forgotten about her dance partner. Forgotten that by tying herself so closely to the Song, she'd left herself open to its influence.

The Song was alive. Not embodied like her, but alive all the same, and driven to grand purpose likely beyond mortal understanding. It had followed her lead in the dance, but it had entered her spirit in return.

It lived, breathed, and grew, as though her spirit was nothing more than another Engine. She felt its strength in her limbs and was certain she could stand against a host of senior Singers and still have more control over the Song than them.

It was the cost that concerned her, though, for she was still but a mortal. Barely a woman grown, and the strength of the Song was so, so much greater than her own.

She shivered again, the same question running through her mind that had been running through it ever since she'd broken apart from Nightkeep's Engine as they fled on Tanwen's back.

What would happen to her as the Song continued to grow within her spirit?

The door to the Engine room opened, and she wasn't surprised to find Orenil was the one who entered. He glanced briefly around, then made straight for the alcove. He stopped as soon as she was in sight. "Do you want to talk about it, or would you prefer to be left alone?"

That he knew her well enough to ask softened the

shield she'd built around her heart. She patted the bench next to her and he sat down. She shifted so that their shoulders were touching and she could lean her head against his shoulder. He took her hand in his own and listened as she shared her fears.

When she was done, all he said was, "Whatever happens, I'll be here, and if there's anything you need, I'll give it if I can."

The ice in her veins thawed, and her breath came easier. She closed her eyes and relaxed.

They sat in silence, their spirits lulled to rest by the Engine as the darkness gathered in the lands beyond.

16

Radyn nearly jumped out of his skin when he practically ran into Kaya. He'd been too lost in his thoughts, too deep in reflection, to pay attention to where he was going or who was in his way. Kaya, coming from the direction of the Engine room, seemed no better. He'd turned a corner and jumped to the side to avoid her.

She was equally startled, and looked sheepishly down at her feet. "Sorry, I wasn't paying much attention."

"No apologies necessary." He took her in at a glance. She had her arms wrapped tightly around her as though she were cold, though the warmth of the late autumn air lingered in the hall. She kept her eyes locked on her feet, her thoughts in a place not here or now.

Questions leaped to his lips, but the sight of her froze them on his tongue. After all she'd been through, the questions could wait. "I'm sorry. I was so eager to see Aria, I didn't even stop to check on you."

"Don't be. I didn't mind. It was important for me to get some time to myself."

"How are you now?"

She gave a small shrug, then finally looked up and met his gaze. "To tell you the truth, I'm not sure, but I'm well enough to meet with Jyn and the others."

"Someone found you, too?" A junior Dagger had found Radyn a moment after he'd stepped from his door.

Kaya inclined her head. "Shall we?"

"It would be my honor." Radyn offered Kaya his arm, and after a moment's hesitation, she took it. Her hand trembled against his bicep, and he looked at her, but she looked studiously away. He briefly considered asking, but given her look, decided against it. What she chose to share or not would be her choice when she was ready.

The journey to the council chambers didn't take long, leaving Radyn wishing they could delay. Kaya's hand was heavy on his arm. The Dagger standing guard at the door let them in to a debate already in full swing.

One of Jyn's senior Swords was on his feet. "We sacrificed nearly half our warriors! To what end?"

He sealed his lips when he noticed the new arrivals. He straightened out his uniform, then sat down. Radyn ignored the question, for it wasn't his to answer. The question had been directed at the Blade.

Jyn, both peacemaker and warrior, found the narrow path between the rudeness of his Sword's complaint and the uncomfortable truth it accurately summarized. He gestured for Radyn and Kaya to join them, then said, "I apologize that I can't give you more time to recover from your ordeal, but the nuddu's advance is relentless. We risked the warriors we did because we believed that any hope we have lies in you. I hope you can tell us our efforts will be worth the steep cost we paid."

Radyn turned slightly in his seat so he could search Kaya's expressions and posture for any hint of what bothered her. She still wore the muddy and torn clothing she'd worn throughout her brief captivity, but she sat at the table as though she were Firestone's Master of the Song, expecting the respect she was due.

She'd grown so much since he'd rescued her from Nightkeep's plots. He wished her life could have been easier, but the never-ending challenges had served as a white-hot forge that had shaped her into one of the strongest and most capable people he'd ever met.

Perhaps even more impressive was what her trials hadn't stolen from her. Exhaustion and lack of sleep revealed themselves in the drawn lines of her face, but she still met every questioning gaze with a compassion that quenched the anger many of the warriors around the table felt as they weighed the loss of so many of their closest friends against her presence. When she spoke, her voice left no doubt in the listeners that she understood their feelings. "I am humbled, truly, to be here. I have long known that Firestone's Manirah were uncommonly honorable, but I never imagined so many would sacrifice so much on my behalf. You have my word that I will do everything in my power to justify the sacrifice."

Jyn dipped his head in her direction and held the slight bow. "You honor us, Kaya, but please don't attribute to nobility what was more accurately an act of desperation and self-preservation. The question remains: Is there a way to save us from the nuddu?"

Kaya sat with the question while the others silently leaned forward. Radyn's ever-present connection with his shards allowed him to sense the subtle vibrations in the Song that danced around the woman he loved like a daughter. He lacked the sensitivity to guess the nature of her exploration, but her search didn't take long.

"I believe I can help, although I don't think you'll like my solution."

Jyn spread his arms out wide. "At this point, any option besides certain death is welcome."

"I believe I can get Firestone in the air again," Kaya said.

Her claim set off a cacophony of responses, a reaction she'd no doubt expected, for she made no attempt to elaborate, but leaned back in her chair as the objections and questions washed over her.

Radyn, too, ignored the cries, arguments, and questions the council members lobbed like arrows into the sky. His gaze remained fixed on Kaya.

She feigned a confident indifference, but a moment of study revealed a deep resignation, as though she'd just made a choice between two unsavory futures. He promised himself he would ask, but later, when they could speak in private.

Jyn stood to quiet the half-dozen conversations that fought for dominance. Once he had everyone's attention, he began a more orderly interrogation. "You're sure of this?"

"Not sure, but confident."

"Why didn't you let us know of this ability earlier?"

Radyn started to object at Jyn's hostile tone, but Kaya's hand brushing against his silenced him. Not everyone around the table shared his opinion of Kaya's worth, especially now. Singers had always cloaked themselves in a shroud of mystery. Swords and Daggers, who by the nature of their duty obsessed with the more pragmatic aspects of the Song, tended to view Singers with some mix of respect, awe, and suspicion. How much more potent would that mix be regarding Kaya, whom other Singers treated the way most clan warriors treated them? Better to address the doubts, especially if the fate of Firestone hung in the balance.

"I only became convinced I could perform such a healing earlier today. Before, I thought I was limited to the slow process of healing I used to bring Underhill's Engine back to full strength."

"What changed?" Jyn asked.

"Our flight from the shadow shrine earlier, and more specifically, our escape from Nightkeep's dragons, forced me to attempt a feat I've never dared try before. I sang, alone, to a healthy Engine."

Radyn limited his surprise to furious blinking, but the Singers around the table erupted in objections. They were almost echoes of one another, all shouting that what she claimed was impossible.

Radyn crossed his arms as his thoughts turned inward. The skepticism was more than justified. One of the Singers' first and strongest rules was that none were allowed to sing to the Engine alone. Common understanding was that the strength of the Song running through an Engine was simply too great for any single individual to endure.

Personal experience supported the claim. Radyn had connected once, many years ago, with an Engine that was nearly dead, and even that fragment of power had almost been enough to kill him. Everyone he knew that had connected to an Engine alone, from Elora to Magni's wife, was killed in the attempt. For all Kaya had accomplished, even this seemed too much.

But this was Kaya, and what point would she have to lie?

Unless…

Jyn's thoughts must have traveled in the same direction, for he held up a hand to forestall the objections that spread throughout the room. "Before we continue, I think it would be wise if we could examine you for any trace of shadow. Do you consent?"

Kaya acquiesced without hesitation, like one who had predicted the request and resigned herself to it.

Several Singers, two healers, and Radyn all took turns placing their hands on her shoulder and searching her body and spirit for any trace of shadow. One by one they acknowledged that they could find nothing, but Radyn didn't feel confident until his own thorough search revealed nothing but the Song in her spirit, louder and clearer than he'd ever heard it.

She'd emerged from her captivity, as she emerged from all of her trials, stronger than before. Perhaps her claim wasn't as impossible as it seemed.

Satisfied, Jyn asked, "This seems as good a time as any to ask about our flight. Nightkeep abandoned a pursuit that would have almost certainly left them victorious. Why?"

"I sang to one of Nightkeep's Engines and caused it to drop, just a little, the same as the 'Little Fall' I've heard about from Firestone's past. Nightkeep's Singers couldn't stop me, and they called off the pursuit before I had to make good on my threat."

The explanation stunned every tongue to silence, and Radyn's was no exception. He believed that his pride in her abilities was second to no one, but he still sometimes had nightmares about the 'Little Fall,' the terrible moment that pitch darkness that had swallowed him whole. Twice in his life, he'd had every comforting lie of his childhood stripped from him. First when his father died, then again when the city he'd always trusted fell.

Now Kaya confessed she'd done the same, intentionally, to another city. Even to protect their lives, it seemed a step too far, like she'd crossed a line that she couldn't return from.

Of course, this was why Nightkeep had wanted her all those years ago. It was probably why the Seer had wanted her at the shadow shrine. By the gate, it was why he and Aria had been forced to exile themselves from Firestone. Somehow it still caught him by surprise.

Jyn leaned back in his chair as he absorbed yet another perspective-shifting revelation.

Radyn's thoughts raced ahead. Once word spread of what had happened, how would the other cities react? If Nightkeep wanted allies, Kaya had handed them a unifying tale that would serve admirably.

Jyn ran his hand down his face. "Right. We'll need to return to that. Let's say you're telling the truth. You can heal Firestone's Engine in time to get it back in the sky. What good does that do us? We still don't have enough time to evacuate Underhill, and I won't abandon some fraction of the population unless I have no choice."

"How you divide up the people is up to you," Kaya said. "Once I heal the Engine, I'll need a team of Singers to fly Firestone. The nuddu are attracted to the Engines. My idea was to use Firestone as a diversion. It captures the nuddu's attention while a team of Singers here briefly shuts down Underhill's Engine. We draw the nuddu away."

Magni, who'd been reasonably silent throughout the council, spoke for the first time. "But do we know the nuddu will follow Firestone? They didn't attack Nightkeep."

Kaya's first uncertainty passed over her face. "To that, I'm afraid I have no certain answer. I'd hoped to find something in the Song channeled by Nightkeep's Engines, but they seemed exactly as they had growing up. I suspect the nuddu didn't avoid Nightkeep because of something the Singers did, but for another reason."

"Any idea what that reason might be?" Magni pressed.

"Not with any certainty. It could be they're being controlled, or that something else has finally driven them beyond the equatorial boundaries. I couldn't say."

Jyn had heard enough. He'd always been a decisive man, a characteristic that befitted all who rose to the rank of Blade. "I believe we would be wise to split our population. Magni, how many people do you estimate we can safely get to Firestone and provide supplies for?"

The giant tapped his fingers against the table as he thought. "Say about a third of our population. Maybe a bit less."

"Arrange it. Divide people up so that if either Firestone or Underhill falls, the other still has the best chance of success." The Blade turned to Radyn. "Take Tanwen and fly Kaya to Firestone. Protect her until we can get more Swords over there."

Radyn was almost compelled to remind Jyn that he no longer obeyed the Blade's commands, but held his tongue. In this case, he would have insisted on the duty anyway.

Jyn finished giving out his first round of orders, then dismissed the group. "Ladies and gentlemen, get to it. Kaya has given us a chance. Let's make sure we make the most of it."

17

The storm passing over the forest had thinned to a light mist, allowing the Seer to spot the shadow of the dragon as it fell toward them. He fought his way through the muck around the fallen dragon, ignored by the shadow warriors, until he reached the clearing. He only beat his guest's arrival by a minute. This dragon, like the fallen one that had sacrificed itself for Firestone, was an elder, scales darker than a moonless night, gleaming like a freshly polished sword.

The warriors of Nightkeep leaped from the dragon's back, landing softly in the mud and forming a perimeter to protect their Blade.

She jumped down a moment later, her landing making the others' look downright clumsy. The Seer swallowed his pride in service of his mission and bowed. He held the pose a moment longer than was comfortable, then rose and met her gaze.

Only a fool would doubt Lynae's capability. She was the youngest Sword to be elevated to the role of Nightkeep's Blade, and was perhaps one of the youngest serving Blades in the history of the cities. Even standing still, she seemed like she was never more than a heartbeat away from violence. The Song wasn't as strong around her as someone like Jyn or Radyn, but that didn't make her weak. Rumor had it that no Sword in Nightkeep had beaten her in sparring in almost two years. Golden hair was tied back tightly, and she surveyed the battlefield with cold precision.

Her voice was like an icy hand pressed against the bottom of his spine. "You've been busy."

"Firestone's response surprised me."

A small snarl escaped her control. "You and me both. Jyn has a reputation as a considered leader and a careful man. I didn't expect him to send almost every dragon and Manirah down your throat. I take it the girl was rescued?"

"To my dismay, yes."

Lynae's eyes narrowed. "How did they reach her? It's unlike you to make a mistake."

The truth galled, but he didn't avoid it. "Jyn wasn't the only one I underestimated. Before the raid, I'd spoken with the girl and infected her with shadow. It had hooks deep in her spirit when I left, and she was cut off from the Song. It should have been impossible for her to banish it from her spirit. I figured that even if they reached her room, they'd only discover another servant of shadow. Both Belzrak and I believed the defense of the shrine was more important."

A slight exaggeration, but close enough to the truth it would withstand questioning. He hadn't known if shadow had taken her spirit, but it should have still been a part of her. Regardless, he'd chosen to defend the shrine instead of her, for his master's command had been clear. Now he wasn't so sure.

"The girl is a problem," Lynae said, echoing the Seer's thoughts perfectly.

"Strong as she is, she's no threat on her own."

He didn't see the blow that snapped his head around. His vision swam, then steadied. He put his hands on his knees until he felt steady again.

Damn all the Manirah. Lynae would pay. They'd all pay, even those he counted among his allies. Not today, but soon. He cursed and put a lid on his anger, then straightened.

"Not a threat?" Lynae snapped. "She sang, by herself, to one of my Engines and threatened to drop an entire city."

The Seer paled. "Impossible. Even for her. I was in a room with her. She's not that strong."

Lynae snorted. "For someone who calls himself 'the Seer,' you're as blind as that poor dragon's corpse." She gestured at Firestone's elder, and when the Seer turned, he saw the other golden eye had been removed. Those that had taken it licked their lips, as though they were staring at their next meal.

Nightkeep's Blade pointed at the dragon she'd ridden in on. "No point in us arguing now. He's summoned you."

The Seer shook his head. "I shouldn't be away from the shrine, not now."

"Not up to me, and it isn't a request."

The Seer glanced back at the tree where the shrine was hidden, wondering if there was some way he could escape the summons. None occurred to him.

"May I bring the shrine up to Nightkeep with me?"

"If it's as powerful as you've been telling us, then that's also a decision I can't make alone, so no. Now get on the dragon."

Lynae was a useful ally, but her first loyalty was always to Nightkeep, and if she was given an order, she would follow it. Any argument was as good as trying to knock down a wall with a spoon. "Fine. Hopefully, it's quick."

Lynae shook her head. "It will take as long as it takes, and be grateful I'm not hauling you up in chains because, I assure you, the possibility was thoroughly discussed."

***

THE SEER's stomach lurched as the dragon leaped into the air and continued its acrobatics for the duration of the brief flight. Though the dragon had done little more than carry them higher along a reasonably straight heading, he disembarked feeling as though he'd been twisted, flipped, and dropped. Those Manirah who claimed to enjoy flight were either liars or deeply broken, for humans were not meant for flight. They were of the land, and it was to the land they should have remained attached. His ancestors' first sin, and the one they were still paying for today, was that they had reached for stars that didn't belong to them.

He regained his composure quickly enough. Lynae's eyes would watch him constantly, seeking the weakness with which she could pry him away from her precious city. She'd no doubt considered throwing him from the dragon on their ascent and claiming he'd been killed in the battle. It wasn't mercy that stayed her hand, but uncertainty. She might hate him, but she wouldn't move against him until she was sure Nightkeep had no need of him. He couldn't afford to give her reason, not when his life's work was so close to completion.

They left behind the tall walls of Nightkeep's Nest and entered the fields that consumed the rest of the surface of the city. Wider and flatter than most of the Makers' cities, Nightkeep boasted more arable land per citizen than any other city, which was the very foundation of the city's strength. Today, the farmers were busy with the late season harvest, their skin darkened from regular exposure to the sun.

Work stopped as Lynae passed. Farmers covered in sweat and soil bent their knees and bowed as their Blade strode down the well-worn paths between fields. Lynae didn't acknowledge their presence, but none dared to rise again until she was well past.

They came to a door which opened up onto a stairwell, guarded by two diligent junior Daggers who bowed at the waist as Lynae swept between them. The Seer almost had to take the steps two at a time to keep up with the Blade's demanding pace.

The hallways immediately below the surface were a hive of activity. Here the harvest from the surface above was sorted and processed, with nothing going to waste. Many of those working here today were temporary, only rising to the surface during the harvest months before returning to the bowels of the city once the process was completed. Skin tones were lighter here, as many only visited the surface as often as was mandated by the Nightkeep elders.

He and Lynae continued their descent into the very heart of Nightkeep. After more than a month on the surface, the familiar routines and surroundings jarred the Seer into revelation.

Yes, the Makers' cities had allowed humanity to survive, but not in any manner worthy of life. He'd grown used to the curving and chaotic lines of a tree's bark, the uncertainty of tomorrow's weather, and the constantly uneven ground beneath his boots. He'd cursed the wilderness plenty the last few weeks, but only in its absence did he understand that it had been a home to him in a way no city ever had. Humans didn't belong to this world of regimented routine, narrow hallways, and smooth decks.

Humanity had come from the dust, and it was to the dust they should return.

They stopped outside a nondescript door. Two senior Swords stood guard.

"He's in?" Lynae asked.

The Swords nodded in unison, then stepped to the side so that she and the Seer could enter. Both cast questioning looks at him as he passed, for his face was only known to a few in this city.

Let them question. Too many equated power with publicity, but real control was shaping the course of events from the shadows, a technique he'd learned from his master.

Their arrival transformed a small study into a claustrophobic cell. Papers were scattered in every corner, and a small bookshelf pressed itself against one wall as though it were frightened. A teapot rested precariously on a pile of papers that looked ready to fall from the top shelf at the slightest provocation.

Semuel, Nightkeep's venerable Elder, locked steely gray eyes on the arrivals, then gestured for them to find seating.

Lynae kicked aside a pile of books to reveal a cushion she could kneel on, and the Seer, after a fruitless search, settled himself on the floor.

It would be an easy mistake to underestimate Semuel, given the state of his study. Chaotic surroundings aside, his wits were as sharp as a butcher's blade, honed by years of difficult decisions. He and Lynae worked in tandem to guide Nightkeep's future, and much of its success these last ten years was due to this man's guidance.

Semuel's position was unique among the cities. Nightkeep's Elder had no equivalent in any of the other clans. The responsibilities Semuel assumed were held by the Blades elsewhere, but Nightkeep's size and population meant no Blade could handle the scope of civic duties that were required to run the city. The Elder was their solution.

The Elder was always chosen from the ranks of the clan, which minimized the chances the Elder and the Blade's priorities would diverge too greatly. They would always be products of the same training system, and were usually children raised with the same worldview. In Nightkeep, the Blade ruled the clan and the Manirah, but the Elder ruled the population. Shields reported directly to Semuel, allowing Lynae to focus her attention entirely on her massive number of Swords and Daggers. It had served Nightkeep well. It had also kept the Seer alive, as Semuel found his arguments more persuasive than Lynae did.

Would he still, after what Lynae had revealed to the Seer?

Semuel fixed the Seer with a stare that would have drawn blood if it could. "When I heard the first whispers of you, I didn't believe a word of them."

The Seer kept his deepest thoughts separated from his expressions, for the rumors Semuel had stumbled upon had been carefully laid by the Seer's servants. Semuel still believed he had found the Seer, where the truth was the Seer had gradually reeled him in, a fish that didn't realize it had been caught. He let Semuel continue.

"In time, I came to believe you were on to something. I'm still not sure that I can bring myself to believe all that you claim, but until today you've proven yourself time and time again, and you've earned a measure of my trust."

Semuel paused. "That trust is close to breaking for good. One of my cities almost fell from the sky today, and the battle that was supposed to solidify Nightkeep's future has instead failed, our Manirah forced to retreat without so much as a fight. What happened?"

The flight to Nightkeep had given the Seer time to consider his response to the predictable question. He found his refuge in the truth, as he always did. "The girl happened. She did the impossible, twice in one day."

Semuel wasn't placated. "I've cooperated with you because, until today, you seemed to have a solid grasp of the impossible."

"No, you've cooperated because I possess knowledge and skills that you don't, and our cooperation is mutually beneficial. I fear you're falling into the same trap that led to my followers calling me the 'Seer.' Despite the title, I cannot peer into the future any more than you. Yes, I understand the forces that shape this world better than most, but that doesn't make me infallible."

"If you're not infallible, then what use are you to me?" Semuel snapped.

Lynae's fingers twitched near the hilt of her maniblade, barely containing her eagerness to cut him down.

Fools.

He didn't rise to the level of Semuel's outburst, unwilling to demean himself with uncontrolled emotion.

He sighed, as though he was dealing with obstinate children, and Lynae grasped her hilt. "My proposal is the same that it has been since you first found me. This world seeks balance, which means wiping out a fair portion of the people who remain. The Song of the Engines is fading, and the world doesn't care who dies, so long as the balance is restored. My word to you was that I would ensure that those who survive are the citizens of Nightkeep, and that word remains. I was surprised today, but won't be again. The nuddu are still on the hunt, and Underhill and

Firestone will be the first to fall, followed soon after by the other cities. Kaya has shown an incredible and rare gift, and I'd hoped she would see reason. Unfortunately, she's become feral and dangerous, going so far as to attack her father when he tried to bring her home. If the nuddu don't kill her, I will have to personally."

Lynae snorted at the boast, but a cool glance from Semuel stifled any further outburst. They worked well together, the Seer decided. Both possessed the intelligence their roles demanded, but her passion and his foresight, combined with their respect for one another, made them a dangerous duo. If they ever realized the depths of his deceit, he'd be rightfully worried.

That day wouldn't be today, though. He already saw it in Semuel's eyes. The movement of the nuddu forced his hand, for they would, in time, threaten Nightkeep, and the Seer was the only protection.

"Then what do you propose we do next?" Semuel asked.

"The nuddu have broken the bonds of their confinement and are on the hunt. Although I believe shadow will continue to protect us, I would suggest that the shrine is no longer safe where it is. I should return to the surface and then bring it back to Nightkeep. Then we will be free to move once again, and the nuddu will never come close."

Semuel and Lynae looked at one another, and such was the nature of their working relationship that there was no need to debate. Lynae inclined her head, for there was no other reasonable choice, and Semuel soon agreed. "Very well. We shall do as you suggest, but for your sake, let us hope you are never again as surprised as you were today."

The Seer refused all alcohol, for it served as a barrier

between him and his master, but if he did imbibe, he would have raised a toast to the sentiment.

Kaya had surprised him today, but he would ensure she didn't live long enough to repeat the feat.

18

Kaya rode on Tanwen, sitting behind Radyn as they approached the hills where she'd landed Firestone half a year ago. Half a dozen Singers, including Orenil, who'd been among the first to volunteer, rode in a basket carried in the dragon's claws. If Tanwen was bothered by the incredible weight he carried, he gave no outward sign. The dragon's strength would be tested in the coming days as he made this flight dozens of times, burdened on each repetition with both humans and supplies.

The dead elder dragon in the bog weighed heavy in her thoughts. She felt so small on Tanwen's back, feeling how effortlessly he carried basket and rider. What was she to the dragons that they'd risk their lives for hers? No matter how she considered the matter, it seemed a poor trade.

Her first sight of Firestone in the distance buoyed her sinking feelings. Her life might be a poor trade for a dragon's, but if she could find a way to lift Firestone into the sky, she'd consider it a step toward paying off the debt the dragon's sacrifice had created in the ledger of her heart.

The enormous city seemed smaller now that it was grounded, surrounded by hills that stood taller than it and hid the majority of its bulk. The city couldn't hope to match its surroundings, its surface unnaturally flat in the middle of the tall rolling hills that occasionally stretched into rockier and more jagged peaks. A gap far wider than any human could leap separated the edge of the city from the natural hills, a physical divider that had prevented any curious animals from making a new home.

The size of the Maker constructions stole her breath away, no matter how many times she witnessed them. Firestone wasn't as large as Nightkeep's main city, but it was still an enormous structure, a mountain hollowed out and turned into a home. That it even had a place where it could come to rest defied easy belief, but it fit into the hole in the hills like a hand in a glove.

Tanwen placed the basket down gently, then landed his bulk fifty paces away. The dragon had chosen to land within Firestone's Nest, though there was no reason he couldn't have landed anywhere else. Tradition remained a powerful force, even among the dragons.

Kaya thanked Tanwen as she dismounted. While the Singers unlatched the basket and began climbing out, Radyn said, "As far as I'm concerned, I'm following your orders. What do you need from me?"

She glanced toward the basket as the door on the side opened. "To get started, I'll need privacy. Have them return to their apartments in the Singers' neighborhood so they'll be well out of the way. I'll examine the Engine, then report back to them tonight."

Radyn bowed, then hurried to the basket to head off the Singers. Kaya silently thanked him, then found the nearest stairwell and started the journey toward Firestone's Engine.

She'd never really known this city when it had been flying, though its design was similar enough to the Nightkeep city she'd grown up on that an unearned sense of familiarity pervaded the silent hallways. It had never been her home, but she'd grown intimately acquainted with its Engine all the same.

The shadow rituals performed within Firestone's walls still stained her perception of the place, lingering long after all other life had fled. The hallways weren't merely quiet, but dead and lifeless, and a shiver ran down her spine as she wondered if anyone would feel truly comfortable living here again. Firestone had fallen, breaking the implied promise of the city, and she didn't know if that trust could ever be repaired.

Kaya opened the doors to the Engine room and stepped inside, ensuring they were sealed behind her. She didn't think any of the Singers would attempt to follow her while she was working, but it was better to be safe than to endure their interference. When it came to healing the Engine, she only needed their strength. She could do without their attempts at skill.

The lantern she carried was the only light in the room, and it reflected off the perfectly cut angles of the Engine. Though it lacked the inner light of the Song, the stone was beautiful on its own, even in reflected light. She wandered around the walkway and found the balcony that reached closest to the Engine. She put down the lantern and sat.

Once her heart and breathing were settled, she closed her eyes and reached out to the Engine. Its Song still played within, weak and distant, as though it were miles away and carried by a faint breeze. Shadow had pierced the Engine the same way the Seer had pierced her. It had set its hooks in deep and clawed against the Song, choking much of the light and life out of the Engine. It hadn't killed the Song, only weakened it to the point even most Singers couldn't hear it.

Satisfied that nothing had changed since her last visit, Kaya broke apart from the trance and held the lantern high. Under its light, she saw the spidery cracks deep within the stone, the physical embodiment of the shadow song's disease. Before she could restore the Song to the Engine, she needed to heal the Engine itself. Her progress had been slow before, and she'd expected to need at least another month, but then life had taken a new turn, revealed to her abilities she hadn't known she had before.

It made her wonder about purpose and fate. Humans were nothing if not creatures of story, but was it a coincidence she'd been captured and forced to strengthen her skills to survive, right when Firestone needed her most? Probably, but the Song's roots stretched deep, and she couldn't help but entertain the notion the events and suffering she'd endured had a purpose. If nothing else, the thought brought her a measure of comfort.

She reached out and touched the quiet Engine, then closed her eyes and let the Song fill her body. It leaped to obey, crashing and breaking within her spirit like a lake churned to froth by a summer storm. The stone warmed beneath her fingertips, and for the beat of a heart, if felt as though her hand was pressed against living flesh.

She'd felt the same before. The Engine, she believed, didn't fit into the neat categories of "alive" and "dead" they taught to children. It was a stone, a gem of enormous size, but it was alive, too, granted spirit by a Song whose plan remained far beyond Kaya's understanding.

Last spring she'd discovered that she could grow the Engines, a process not dissimilar to the ones healers used to close cuts with fresh skin. The process had been slow before, limited by the meager amount of Song her body had to work with. Now she could push harder, accomplish in minutes what had once taken her days.

She sang a song of birth, one that echoed the seed sprouting into new bloom or a child growing in the womb. The gem heard the song and repeated it back, for its nature was life. It needed only strength and guidance. She sang until her focus wavered, and then she let the tune fade from her spirit. The gem's warmth fled from under her hand until her hand was only pressed against stone once again.

Kaya opened her eyes, reached down, and picked the lantern up to examine the Engine.

Under the light of the lantern, the truth was plain to see: the dark cracks embedded in the stone had healed. Not completely, but they were smaller than before, and considerably so.

There was a long way left to go, but maybe, just maybe, they'd get Firestone back into the air in time to save them from the nuddu.

Day passed into night, and for the second time that week, Kaya found herself in a small room locked away from the rise and fall of the sun. She wasn't alone, though the Singers likely wished she was. She'd used their strength roughly. They lay scattered around the Engine room like discarded toys. Their labored breathing served as evidence they yet lived, but Kaya had no choice but to continue drawing upon their gifts.

Her focus wavered, and the Song rang a discordant note. Previous experience had taught her not to push beyond this point. The line between healing and injury was as thin as a fingernail. When she'd pushed too hard earlier, she'd cracked open a fracture in the gem she'd just finished healing.

That had been the lowest point of the process yet. Mistakes cost them time and strength, and they had neither to spare. The Singers, already worn, had come close to rebelling.

Orenil had turned the tide of that near-mutiny. He'd spoken of duty and the need to save Firestone's citizens from the nuddu, but it wasn't his words that had changed the Singers' minds. It had been his determination and willingness to sacrifice himself for Firestone's citizens. He'd made the other Singers hesitate, and in that hesitation Kaya had recovered her focus and pulled their spirits into harmony with hers, unwilling to waste the time and breath fighting them.

Since then, they'd been too exhausted to argue. Too much of the Song ran through them, burning them like candles near the end of their wicks. Most resided in the liminal space between awareness and sleep, denied both activity and rest. It was a cruel use Kaya regretted, but necessity stripped any other choice from her.

She let go of the Engine and wobbled on her feet. She grabbed hold of the railing until the weakness passed, then reached down and hauled the lantern higher. The cracks within the Engine were nearly healed, barely visible to her sight. Once more, if she could maintain the focus long enough. Twice at the most.

She glanced around the room, trying to judge the ability of the Singers to support her. Their awkward positions made them look more dead than alive, slumped against railings and walls as though a careless mover had thrown them wherever was most convenient. Most had fallen from standing, and she didn't have the strength to arrange them in more comfortable ways. Mercy demanded she release them from their duty, but again, necessity forced her hand.

She didn't dare sit or close her eyes, but she slumped over the railing as she caught her breath and let her mind rest.

Orenil's voice nearly made her jump out of her skin, as it came from a throat that sounded much older than the young man she cared so deeply for. "Is it done?"

"Not yet. Once more, hopefully."

Orenil shifted. "If I don't survive, know that I have no regrets. I go to the gate willingly."

"I'm not going to let you die doing this."

"Regardless."

She would have said more, but his breathing had steadied as he slipped closer to sleep. Apologies and explanations could wait until she was done. She let all her thoughts drift away, mind and spirit as close to rest as she dared let them. When she felt the strength to carry on, she just reached out and touched the stone again.

She sang of healing and rebirth, the Singers' spiritual voices joined to hers in unwilling harmony, and the Engine responded.

The last of the cracks healed, and the Song ran through the Engine unimpeded. There was no need to peer around the stone with a lantern, for the difference was as clear as day. She released the other Singers from their duty but remained connected to the Engine. Her body and spirit demanded rest, but she couldn't take a break when the end was so close.

She dove deeper into the Engine, finding the Song that resided deep within, close to the limits of her sharp hearing. This Engine wasn't as familiar to her as

Nightkeep's, but that didn't prevent her from inviting the Engine to dance with her spirit. The Song was stronger in her than in the stone, but as their powers entwined, the Song flowed through her into the stone. Like motes of dust swept into a corner, shreds of power collected and grew into something larger, something more powerful and gorgeous than she could have created on her own.

The process was painstakingly slow, but scrap by scrap, she fed the flame of the Song, until the moment when it burst into flame and grew of its own accord, expanding beyond her ability to control or guide.

Kaya separated her spirit from the Engine. In her exhausted condition, the unfiltered strength of the Engine would overwhelm her in moments. She opened her eyes in time to see the first flicker of blue light deep within the heart of the repaired stone. It sparked and burned, racing around the gem like a hummingbird exploring the limits of its environment before settling in the very center.

Pale blue light exploded from the heart of the gem, filling the Engine room with a familiar, welcoming glow. Kaya grinned at the reinvigorated Engine, then collapsed onto her rear, unable to even summon the strength to stand.

Once the Singers were recovered, Firestone could take to the skies again.

19

R adyn loaded the last of the crates into the cradle Tanwen would carry to Firestone and made certain it was secured tightly. Satisfied the food stores wouldn't shift during the flight, he closed the gate of the cradle and bolted it shut. The cradle was shaped from the same alloy found in every corner of a Makers' city, thin enough the weight was no more than necessary, but large enough to carry a cart's worth of anything that needed carrying. He tested the gate to ensure it wouldn't open in flight, then wiped the sweat from his brow. He took a few steps and sat to enjoy a brief respite.

The harvested fields just beyond Underhill's main gate were filled with men, women, and children. Most helped carry supplies from Underhill to the waiting cradles, but a few took what rest they required after pushing their bodies to the brink of exhaustion. The sun blazed hot for this time of year, but better that than rain, mud, or snow.

The preparations neared their conclusion, and with not a moment to spare. The most recent reports from scouts claimed that the nuddu were expected by nightfall, and the sun seemed all too eager to drop from its zenith below the horizon. Even so, they would be in time. When he and Tanwen had left Firestone last, Kaya, Orenil, and the other Singers had all been resting. The Engine glowed again, bright as Radyn had ever seen it. Lifting the city would be no problem, and with any luck, they'd drag the nuddu after them.

Kaya had done the impossible again.

Those who weren't working on loading the cradles prepared Underhill for the quieting of its Engine. Radyn had never seen the technique performed, though Kaya had assured him the Firestone Singers were up to the task. The Singers would reduce the amount of Song flowing through the Engine to a bare trickle, just enough to keep the gem connected to the Song and to keep fans and exhausts running.

Underhill had an unpleasant few days ahead, but so long as the nuddu left the surface ruins alone, they'd be remembered as nothing more than an annoyance.

A shadow fell over Radyn and he looked up. "Resting already?" Aria asked.

Radyn pushed himself to his feet. "They're almost done loading the last cradles. We'll make one last flight, and we should be done."

He left the rest unspoken, for the next flight would separate the two of them. For how long, no one knew. With luck, no more than a few days, but a prolonged separation wasn't out of the question. Much depended on the nuddu's behavior.

He held tightly to her hands as he imagined being absent for the birth of his child, and with a lover's intuition, she said, "You'll return in time. I know it."

"I shouldn't be leaving in the first place."

She ran her thumbs across the backs of his hands.

"You're needed there, more than with us." Her voice wavered as she spoke, betraying her true feelings.

"Say the words, and we'll leave it all behind."

Her hands trembled beneath his. "When we were younger, I used to think those were only words. Pretty words you used to tell me how much I mattered to you." She grasped his hands tightly. "They aren't, though, are they?"

"Nothing in this world means more to me than you and our child. Nothing."

A shudder passed through her body. "Without friends and neighbors, it hardly seems like living."

She couldn't bring her gaze to meet his.

"Is that your answer?" he asked, his voice full of mercy.

Aria buried her head in his chest and nodded. "Just come back to us, please."

He held her close, committing the smell of her hair and the feel of her pregnant body to his memory. "I'll do all I can."

THE LAST OF their time together was interrupted by a speck on the northern horizon that grew rapidly larger. Radyn's eyes narrowed and he swore at the sight.

Fortunately he wasn't the only eye keeping watch, and before he could call to Tanwen, one of Firestone's riders was in the air, rushing toward the unexpected visitor.

"You should go," Aria said.

He brought her hand up and brushed his lips lightly against the back of it. "I think I'd rather stay here unless I'm needed."

Aria shook her head, but the blush across her cheeks told Radyn he'd spoken well. They walked hand in hand while Radyn studiously ignored anything happening around Underhill. All too soon, a young clan student came running toward them.

"Told you," Aria said.

He leaned over and kissed her. "You might have been right, but I'd still argue I chose best."

She smiled as their lips parted. "You'll hear no argument here."

The girl arrived, breathless, a moment later. Her face was scrunched up in a look of disgust at the pair. "Miranda and the Blade have both summoned you, senior Sword."

Radyn took his leave of Aria and followed the girl. She led him to one of Jyn's rooms, where Jyn, Miranda, Magni, and a recently returned Veylan stood in awkward silence. Jyn welcomed Radyn. "I asked Veylan to wait until you were here."

The request must have fit Veylan like a noose, for the foreign Sword tugged at the collar of his robes as though it was choking him. His hand kept twitching toward the maniblade at his hip, though he had the self-control not to grasp it.

Jyn gestured for the Sword to begin. "Please."

Veylan launched into his duty without pleasantries. "Is it true Kaya caused one of Nightkeep's Engines to fail for a moment?"

The room went as silent as a crypt at night. Jyn's response, when it finally came, was slow and measured. "What brings you here, Veylan?"

"Answer the question!"

Magni shifted no more than a fraction of a pace, but into a position more between Veylan and Jyn.

"Why?" Jyn asked.

"Don't play games with me! You know perfectly well

why. Now, on your honor as the Blade of Firestone, can Kaya drop cities on her own?"

Jyn waited Veylan out another moment, hoping he would back off from this line of inquiry, but when the Sword remained adamant, Jyn quietly said, "Yes."

Veylan sagged as though Jyn had delivered a blow instead of an answer, as though, even though he'd certainly known the truth before he stepped into this room, he hadn't believed it possible. He stumbled half a step back before regaining his wits, and he shook his head, all formality stripped from him. "Jyn, you fool."

Jyn's own demeanor shifted, less the Blade of Firestone and more one warrior speaking to another. "It hardly matters now, but even she didn't know she possessed the ability before our raid."

"You're right. It doesn't matter. I knew she was gifted and you had high hopes for her, but did you suspect it might come to this?"

Jyn's lack of answer was answer enough, and Veylan remembered himself. He stood up straighter. "Nightkeep has sent messengers to all the cities informing them of Kaya's ability and how she threatened them."

"All while ignoring their connection to the attacks on the Song and the nuddu breaking through their previous boundaries?"

"Semuel and Lynae are placing all the blame at Kaya's feet, Jyn. They're rallying every city to their cause. The nuddu aren't just approaching Underhill. They've broken free across the continent, and cities are panicking. There won't be any safety anymore."

"And Nightkeep offered up our greatest hope as a scapegoat," Jyn finished.

Veylan shook his head. "Greatest hope? Jyn, whatever the truth is, the cities will never allow Kaya to live. That kind of power, it's too great for any city to have. None of us should be able to drop another from the sky."

Radyn stepped directly in front of Veylan. "Threaten her again, and it's your life in danger."

"Radyn, back off," Jyn ordered.

Radyn glared at Veylan, then snarled and pressed his back against the wall.

"Say what you came to say," Jyn told Veylan.

The other Blade glanced at Radyn, then focused on Jyn. "Nightkeep wants her head, and the other cities are in agreement. Surrender her, or we'll have no choice but to resort to more aggressive measures."

Jyn pointed south. "We've got a nuddu less than half a day away, and I need her to help my exhausted Singers get Firestone back into the air. If we don't, both Firestone and Underhill are dead, regardless. I can't just surrender her."

Veylan was a warrior, and he was smart enough not to push a wounded fighter any deeper into a corner. He rubbed at his chin, then said, "My intent isn't to destroy Firestone, not unless you leave me no other choice. I'll allow her to stay with the city until it is safely up in the air, but no longer."

Silence fell over the room, all eyes on Jyn. Radyn stared hard at the Blade. Capitulation destroyed their best hope for surviving the nuddu and the shadow song, but did they have a choice? Jyn could threaten the other cities with Kaya, but Veylan had met her and would know it for a bluff. If pushed into a corner, Kaya still wouldn't drop a city. She didn't possess the cruelty necessary.

Jyn nodded.

Radyn pushed off the wall and pointed an accusing finger at Veylan. "No!" Then he turned to Jyn. "Everyone in Firestone and Underhill owes her their lives, many of us more than once. You can't send her to an executioner."

Jyn weathered Radyn's accusations like a carved granite stone. "What would you have of me? My duty is first and foremost to the well-being of Firestone. It always has been. If I can sacrifice one to save the rest, why would I not make that choice?"

The Blade's tortured answer gave Radyn pause, and he collected himself before answering. "I would never ask you to put Kaya above your duty to Firestone. But you're only thinking of the current threat, an ultimatum given by those who were allies a week ago. No one alive has learned more about the Song than Kaya. If you care not just about the immediate future of Firestone, but about the future of its children and grandchildren, then you'll weigh carefully the knowledge of the Song and the world we'd lose if we lost her. You might avoid this disaster, only to guarantee our doom years from now."

Veylan interjected. "Be wary, Radyn, for the situation is more dire than you realize. Cities and Blades are terrified. Their answer will not come in the form of some fight or battle you might hope to win. If your gambit with Firestone succeeds, they'll use one of their own cities to lead a nuddu here. The more desperate and scared clans are even whispering about abandoning one of the smaller cities and dropping it on Underhill."

The air in the small room grew suddenly cooler. "They would go that far?" Jyn asked.

Veylan stared down at his feet and shifted his weight. "I've met the girl and liked her. She's a person to me, as real as my wife and children, and I believe she wouldn't harm anyone if she didn't have to. But most people don't know her. To them, she's a story, a monster who drops cities from the sky at her command. They're terrified, and not without reason. People can't live with the fear that the cities might drop at any moment on the whims of a young woman who's barely more than a girl. Yes, they'll do anything to stop her, especially now that the nuddu are free and everything they believed is upended."

A sharp gesture from Jyn froze Radyn's objection before he could voice it. "I have your word you'll allow us to get Firestone in the air and away from the nuddu?"

Veylan tapped his fingers against his leg, weighing the various risks, and in that hesitation, Radyn saw to the heart of the other Sword. He trusted Jyn and trusted Kaya, but he was no fool, and he understood all too well what trouble Kaya could cause if the mood struck her. Much hung on trust alone.

After another moment of weighty silence, he said, "You understand the stakes? Any failure here will result in a total war."

Jyn answered the question with the seriousness it deserved. "I understand."

Veylan grimaced, then bowed. "If that's the price of convincing you to acquiesce without a fight, then yes. You have my word. She'll need to be accompanied by a Singer and a Sword at all times, and will be expected to surrender herself once it is determined Firestone is as safe as circumstances allow. I'll volunteer to be the Sword responsible."

Jyn returned the bow. "Tell your masters you're making a mistake, though I doubt they'll listen. She's our best hope for a brighter future."

Veylan's sharp, curt nod was his only answer, and then he strode from the room to return to his masters and summon a Singer to keep an eye on Kaya.

Radyn turned to follow Veylan out.

"Stop, Radyn."

He almost didn't listen, but he clenched his fists and

turned slowly back to the Blade and his guard. He let his glare say all he didn't dare.

Jyn openly met his eyes without hesitation. The Blade didn't hide behind excuses or reasoning, didn't defend himself, for there was nothing to defend. He'd made the only choice he could. And now he gave the only order he could. "You can say goodbye to her, but don't you dare try anything more. I will not condemn thousands on her behalf."

Radyn didn't acknowledge the order. He turned on his heel and left before they found out for sure which of them was the stronger warrior.

20

R adyn hesitated at an intersection. One hallway led to the front gates of Underhill, the echoes of construction audible even at this distance. Once the Engine was shut down, the door would no longer open or close on its own, and so they built a barrier with a door they could operate without the need for the Song. His heart begged his feet to follow that hallway so he could reach Kaya as quickly as possible.

The other passage would eventually lead him back to his apartment. It was quiet and dim, more than half the hallway lanterns turned off to conserve energy as the Singers began the long and careful process of quieting the Engine. Reason and logic urged him down that path, to Aria, who would help him discern the best way forward.

The battle warred within him, below the level of conscious thought, guided by instinct and experience. When at last a victor emerged, Radyn turned down the quiet hallway, his footsteps lost among the clangs and the shouts of the construction in the distance. He opened the door to the apartment and found Aria at her desk, bent over a pile of papers filled with her notes and sketches.

For a moment, he had the privilege of witnessing her completely unguarded. One of her legs was curled up underneath her, and Radyn knew that when she stood, that foot would be asleep. No matter how many times it happened, she never seemed to learn to keep both her feet on the ground. The focus she turned toward the papers she was studying was no less than a Singer wrestling with the Song for the first time, her spirit and mind unified in their determination. Whatever problem she faced, no matter how difficult it might be, wouldn't last long against such a force. Despite everything, he smiled at the sight, for in this small corner of the world, life was still as it should be.

The illusion shattered when she looked up and saw him standing at the door. She rose to her feet, then grimaced as the numb leg complained against its mistreatment. She hurried toward him, and he met her in the middle of the room in a tight embrace. He didn't need to say anything, for she saw enough on his face. "What happened?" she asked, guiding him to the couch.

He explained as they sat down, explaining only the facts, for she would know well enough how he felt. She listened without interruption, though he felt the tension in her arm as he spoke of Jyn's decision.

"I don't know what to do," he confessed. "I thought I'd do anything to save Kaya."

Her fingers entwined in his own, easing some of the burden on his spirit. "You never imagined the choice would look like this."

"How do I weigh the potential of her ability against so many lives?"

Aria's fingers squeezed his own. "Morality doesn't

come with a scale, my love. Nor can we see the future to measure the consequences of our decisions."

"Then what do I do?"

She reached across with her free hand and tapped his chest. "You go to see her. You speak with her, and then you choose the path that seems best to you. It's not so hard, and even if there is no good answer, no right answer, I trust you."

Radyn sat on the couch, unable to lift himself up and hurry to the main gate. Aria nudged him with her shoulder, then leaned in for a kiss.

"Now go. Unless we're ordered to evacuate, I'll be right here."

Radyn kissed her again, then found the strength to stand. "I love you, you know."

"I know. I love you, too. Now get going before it's too late."

Never one to disobey his wife's commands, Radyn hurried out the door and toward the main gate.

HE'D BARELY CLEARED the construction when he ran into Magni. The giant warrior stood between him and Tanwen, his enormous arms crossed. "It would be best if you remained here with Aria, old friend. No good will come from a visit to Firestone."

"You would deny me a chance to say farewell?"

Magni didn't rise to the bait. "I would save you from the temptation that may very well lead us all into disaster."

It was tempting to argue Jyn's choices with Magni, but there was no point and even less time. Magni likely felt the same about the decision as Radyn did. "Will you stop me?"

Magni let out a long sigh and shook his head. "Jyn

asked I do all I can short of violence to prevent you from leaving."

"Then get out of my way."

Magni stepped aside, but as Radyn passed, he asked, "What are you going to do?"

"I don't know. You have to know, though, that I have no desire to see harm come to either Underhill or Firestone."

He left Magni behind, but it didn't stop the giant from getting the last word in, speaking to his back.

"I know. But I also know you're not one to take 'no' for an answer, even if it's the only one that doesn't doom us all."

TANWEN LANDED on a Firestone that was eerily quiet. The last of the supplies had already been loaded, and the people were below, most in their apartments waiting for the city to lift into the sky.

Just before Radyn took the unguarded stairs that would eventually take him to Kaya, a darkened shadow appeared on the horizon. The sight brought him to a stop. A rounded patch of darkness grew and then narrowed until it was a clear approximation of a human head, hundreds of times larger than any skull. The edges of the shadow shifted and wobbled, making it seem as though the monster might collapse into mist with any step.

Radyn hurried down the stairs. With the nuddu this close, Kaya and the other Singers would be in the Engine room. A vibration passed through his feet as the Engine shunted more of its tremendous powers through the conduits the Makers had designed so many years ago.

Kaya stood outside the Engine room, sitting easily in a

chair. Her cheeks had more color than when he'd seen her last, but the bags under her eyes hadn't faded, and she was slow to notice his arrival. It wasn't all exhaustion that haunted her, though. Her eyes had that half-glazed look that stared into the distance that happened when she was absorbed by listening to the Song.

She eventually took notice of him, though, turning languid eyes toward him. She offered a weak smile as a form of greeting. "I'm listening closely, but I think we're going to make it. The Singers are in control, and the Engine is responding well. Better than before, really. It's a special stone. I can understand why the shadow song is so concerned about it."

The comments stopped Radyn in his tracks. "What do you mean?"

"It's not just an Engine anymore. It's become something more, and that scares the shadow song even more than I do."

Just a handful of words, but Radyn felt as though the city was dropping beneath his feet again. Jyn's decision and the weight of lives landed on him like a boulder dropped from a city, and he found it challenging to breathe. "Kaya, what do you mean?"

She smiled wider. "This Engine. I think it's the key to overcoming the shadow song."

"And you can guide it?"

"Maybe. I don't know."

Their discussion was interrupted by the growing vibration beneath their feet. Radyn felt suddenly heavier, then returned to his normal weight.

He couldn't help himself. He grinned. "You did it!"

Kaya's grin almost matched his own. "Well, they did it, but yes, I was able to bring the Engine back to life. They're controlling the flight of the city, though, and have asked in no uncertain terms that I keep myself out of it."

"They don't want your help?"

She shrugged, unbothered by the slight. "I'm not a Firestone Singer."

"You brought their Engine back from the dead."

"Sure, but I'm not one of them. It's not worth worrying about. We have more important problems."

"That's why I've come. Nightkeep has asked for your head, and the other cities are in agreement." He launched into a quick explanation of what had happened, and Kaya listened with impressive nonchalance. She wasn't nearly as bothered as she should have been.

When he was finished, she asked, "How much time do I have?"

He imagined shaking her shoulders and shouting at her, but a glance told him it would do no good. Her thoughts were running along paths he didn't understand. He calmed himself with a long breath, then said, "A day, maybe. Certainly not much more. Veylan will be back with a Singer."

She brushed the news away. "Then we'll have to be quick. There's much I must learn."

She stood and Radyn gaped at her. "That's it? You can't stop the shadow song in a day."

"No, I can't."

"Then you're just going to sacrifice yourself?"

She cocked her head to one side, as though studying a mystery she didn't quite comprehend. "What would you have me do? Given the fear from the other cities, there's no way of saving my life without endangering or killing thousands."

"But we need you!"

"No, we need to master the Song better than the Makers did. I have to learn how to show you the way."

"In a day? Kaya, you aren't talking sense."

She walked away from the Engine room, forcing Radyn to follow her. "I am, you just aren't capable of hearing it right now."

"What am I missing?"

She paused in the hallway and seemed to take pity on him. "It is easier if I show you. Will you come with me?"

Radyn nodded and followed Kaya as she ascended the same stairs he'd just come down. They climbed until they reached the surface, and Kaya continued until she reached the edge, demarcated by a fence that reached almost as high as her head. She looked upon the nuddu, growing larger on the horizon. The creature faced toward Underhill, angled slightly away from Firestone.

Radyn peered over the edge to watch the hills that had been home to Firestone this past half-year fall slowly away. Firestone was perhaps a hundred feet in the air now, but the Singers continued to lift it with all the strength at their command. A little more time would see the bottom of Firestone high enough to clear any of the surrounding hills, but by then, the nuddu would be close to Underhill.

"I think it's about time," Radyn said.

"I'd hoped we'd be higher by now, but you're right. Give me one moment."

Kaya sat in the grass, crossed her legs, and closed her eyes. Radyn leaned against the fence and connected with two of his shards. Enough to sense their plan taking shape, but not so many he was in danger of being overwhelmed. He gripped the fence posts tight enough his knuckles turned white.

Too much of their plan relied on assumptions. Solid

assumptions, backed by experience, but still nothing more than guesses.

If the nuddu didn't turn, he'd be racing back on Tanwen, and he'd curse to the gates any who stood in his way.

Kaya burned more brightly against his senses, the Song within her nearly as powerful as a dragon. Her presence pressed against him, warming the air and banishing the weariness that crept through his bones. He swore he smelled lilacs in bloom.

"Listen carefully," she said.

He connected to two more shards, more than doubling the pressure against his spirit. In exchange, the notes of Kaya's song rang like bells on a crisp winter morning, shivering the fabric of reality with their purity. He could no longer compare her song to the work of the Singers below, the same as one didn't compare the blade of a master swordsmith with the clay moldings of a child.

Kaya sang to the Engine, and the Engine sang back.

Not as a single voice, nor as a fragment of the Song, but as a small chorus, waves of power harmonizing and building to a crescendo greater than any single voice. Radyn's spirit was swept up in the song, carried along and cradled as the power swirled to unimaginable heights. He blinked, and a tear trickled from the corner of his right eye, for the voices that joined with the Engine were familiar.

That was what Kaya was speaking of. The reason Firestone's Engine mattered. The path ahead remained dim, but for the first time, Radyn understood the direction they needed to travel.

Firestone's Engine blazed, its Song reaching Singers across the continent. It rang a note of defiance against the shadow.

Radyn refused to let his gaze upon the nuddu waver. Would it listen?

The nuddu's steps had brought it into the foothills surrounding Underhill. Radyn's grip on the fenceposts tightened further, the wood cracking under his shard-enhanced strength. Their plan hadn't reached its conclusion yet, but if the nuddu didn't change course soon, Radyn would have no choice but to call for Tanwen.

Kaya's song wasn't only the light to attract the moth; it was the signal for the Singers of Underhill to put their Engine to rest. The process had started days ago, leaving the Singers little left to complete. Radyn strained his senses to pick out the song of Underhill's Engine, a faint note against the powerful song of Firestone's Engine.

The soft note faded below the range Radyn could hear even as he tapped into the rest of his shards, baring his spirit to the full strength of Firestone's song for a dangerous moment. He listened closely again, but there was nothing.

Kaya confirmed his sensation. "They've put the Engine to rest."

Radyn disconnected from his shards before Firestone's newfound strength overwhelmed him, and leaned forward. The nuddu took another step toward Underhill. Then another, its progress unchecked. Their plan had failed.

His heart hardened against what he'd soon have to do. Tanwen would be the only possible escape for the citizens and Manirah still trapped in Underhill, and there'd be chaos as Radyn tried to escape with Aria in tow.

He cursed sharply. He'd judged Firestone the more dangerous of the two locations, and he'd been wrong.

Now he'd have to fight through friends and neighbors to save his wife and child.

21

The Seer shifted his weight, seeking comfort among a collection of pillows and mattresses that seemed determined to provide him none. He'd had everything from his previous apartment moved to Nightkeep when he'd successfully recruited both Semuel and Lynae to his cause, but he'd barely gotten settled before he'd finally convinced the surface dwellers to grant him access to one of their shrines. Since then, he'd slept in carts, caves, and within the guest rooms of the shrine, but none had come close to offering him the comfort of the apartment he'd painstakingly arranged before. Even here, the lumps in the pillows were in the wrong places, digging into sagging flesh they should be supporting. He cursed silently and shifted again.

The arrival of the shadow shrine hadn't helped matters. So long as it remained unused, there was little trouble, but the first time he'd connected with it to follow the nuddu's progress, the whole city had begun to tilt. Lynae had stormed into his room with her maniblade lit, eager for his head.

The memory still galled. Despite knowing more of his plans than any other outsider, they continued to look down on him, continued to underestimate both the true power of the shadow song and the depth of his connection with it. He longed for the day when he could reveal his full mastery to them, and imagined over and over the expression on Lynae's face when he killed her with a dark blade of shadow.

The pleasure of the imagining almost distracted his mind from the discomfort of his body. He was softer than he'd once been, focused on the mastery of the shadow song to the exclusion of all else, including the care of his body.

No matter. The incident had been blamed on Kaya, stoking Nightkeep's fervor to even greater heights. Nightkeep had assigned him a new apartment as far away from their Engine as possible. A couple more tests proved he could safely connect with the shrine, so long as certain conditions were met. First, Nightkeep's Singers needed to be made aware of his impending connection, and he couldn't dive too deep into the shadow song. If those conditions were met, the Singers could hold the city steady through his efforts. He wasn't making friends with the exhausted Singers, but the mission continued.

Soon the matter would be concluded. He'd just heard word a bit ago that Veylan had agreed to spare Kaya for as long as was necessary for Firestone to take to the sky. By now, the senior Sword would be flying to Firestone with Presnell to eliminate the shadow song's greatest threat. Better if Kaya was already dead, but she was out of time, and there was nothing more she could do.

The Seer almost laughed, but the presence of the four guards in the room helped keep his mirth in check. That the Blades and Singers would be so eager to kill the one woman who had the slightest chance of disrupting his plans never ceased to delight him. Veylan's foolish honor-bound delay made him want to choke the life out of the Sword, but Kaya had no escape. She'd done an admirable job tying the noose around her neck.

Once he found a position that was as comfortable as any, the Seer placed his hands on either side of the shrine. It was a simple but perfect cube of what appeared to be a black glass or obsidian. Delicate as it appeared, it was as sturdy and unyielding as any stone. Its edges were sharp enough to cut like a blade, a discovery that had almost cost the Seer a finger the first time he picked it up. It appeared as dark as a moonless night, but there were times when he swore the darkness swirled slowly within the cube, more of a shifting ink than the absolute lack of light.

He'd been disappointed when he'd first laid eyes on it, expecting something more aesthetically pleasing, but he'd grown to appreciate its stark simplicity and the perfection of its design. It inspired not by appearance, but by function. Like the shadow song itself, it brought no undue attention to itself.

Every eye in the room turned to him as he shifted one last time. Two of the guards in the room were his best remaining soldiers, capable of manipulating the shadow song with the skill of a Sword. The other two were Belzrak's. The Seer welcomed them with open arms, for they were ultimately obedient to him instead of the Manirah, and would protect him as well as the shrine.

He nodded to let them know he was about to connect, then did so. He dove into the primal power of the song, the emptiness that lay at the heart of creation. Strands of shadow spread from the shrine, the largest of them connecting to the other three shrines scattered across the continent. With this one, he could find the others, but that joy was for another day. Today, he traced one of the familiar strands to the nuddu's spirit far to the north. It neared Underhill's Engine, the ruin's song drawing the nuddu closer.

It was very close now, and wouldn't be long.

Every strand of shadow reverberated at once as Firestone's Engine nearly exploded with energy. The Seer groaned, his spirit tied tightly to the countless weaves of shadow tossed about like leaves before a tornado.

Such strength, and it could only come from one Singer connected to one Engine.

For several long moments, his will was frozen by the sensations coursing through his body. There'd been a time, long before, when he'd been a Singer chasing a feeling just like this, and his body ached with the memories of what he'd once believed was possible.

Kaya stripped two decades from his spirit in less time than it took his heart to beat twice, and even he stared in awe. He'd always believed it was possible, at least until his investigations had made him aware of the shadow song.

His spirit trembled and wavered, balanced precariously on a razor's edge of belief.

With a power like that…

He didn't dare complete the thought, for it would have rendered the last twenty years of his life meaningless.

Not just meaningless.

If what she revealed were true, it made him a monster.

He lashed out, his actions untouched by reason, consideration, or logic. The justifications came easily enough a moment later. She intended to drop Nightkeep! What other need could there be for so much strength?

Instinct led him to pluck the string that connected the shrine in his hands to the nuddu hundreds of miles away. The beast required little convincing. Woven by the master of shadow, they were designed to seek the Engines and destroy them, so the barest hint of encouragement changed its direction.

Underhill wasn't going anywhere. Once the nuddu changed direction, he urged it to hurry. If the city was given too much time, it might slip yet again through his grasp, and he wouldn't allow such a thing. Today was the day. Today, he'd bring down Firestone and Kaya before they could ruin the work of his lifetime.

A FIRM KNOCK on the door pulled the Seer from the trance state that allowed him to manipulate the shadow song. He blinked open his eyes and groaned as the dim light of his room struck like the direct rays of the sun. The more he exposed himself to the forces of shadow, the less pleasant light became. Fortunately, humans had become creatures who shunned the light, and so his pale skin and wide irises didn't attract much attention.

Four dark blades of shadow sprang to life around the room as each of the warriors took a position between the door and the Seer.

"Who is it?" the Seer called, his voice hoarse.

"A messenger from the Singers, sir. They're demanding to see you."

The Seer glanced down at the cube. The nuddu had received its directions, so there was little more need of his direct intervention. Once the nuddu brought down Firestone, it would naturally seek the next closest Engine, which would be Underhill's. The work would be finished soon, regardless of his efforts.

Still, he had no desire to leave the shrine now. Too

much was happening too quickly. "Can it wait until night has fallen?"

"I'm sorry, sir, but they're insistent. Word is that they've sensed something from Firestone."

The Seer removed his hands from the cube, hesitating as though he was tearing himself away from a lover. Soon he would be apart from them, never forced to listen to another unwelcome voice. The day couldn't come soon enough, but it hadn't yet arrived. He sighed and stood up. He hated to leave the room, but if the shrine wasn't safe in Nightkeep's primary city, guarded by four of the most dangerous warriors in the world, it wasn't safe anywhere. "Very well. Give me one moment."

He took the shrine toward a chest made of Makers' steel. The chest was bolted to the decking, and the only key that opened it was on a necklace hanging around his neck. He placed the shrine inside, shut the lid, and locked the chest. The key returned to its rightful place underneath his tunic, the slight weight reassuring against his chest.

The messenger was a stern young man with dark hair. He wore the rank of a senior Dagger, too highly ranked to serve as a messenger for most. He waited at crisp attention while the Seer locked the door, then set a brisk pace. The Seer was familiar enough with the city that he soon determined they were heading toward the Singers' quarters.

He sighed again, preparing himself for a long walk. The Singers, due to the nature of their gifts, were traditionally established near the outer perimeter of a city where the Song of the Engine would disturb them least. Their quarters were on the opposite side of Nightkeep, which meant the Seer would have to cross the entire city to reach their destination.

He was winded by the time he arrived. The Dagger

hadn't been of a mind to let him walk at his typical unhurried pace, and he imagined he looked a mess. He stank of sweat.

There was nothing for it, though. If this was how the Singers wanted to treat him, they deserved the consequences of sharing a small enclosed room. The Dagger opened the door for the Seer, who hadn't even had time to straighten his clothing. He glared at the Dagger as he walked in, but the young man's face was a study in impassiveness.

"About time," Dougan, the Master of the Song for Nightkeep, said. "We've been waiting for what feels like the better part of the day."

The Seer ground his teeth together. The comment was more show than substance, which made it even more annoying. Dougan was a rarity among Singers, for he was pragmatic to the very center of his unshakeable spirit. His sensitivity to the Song was entirely natural, a gift he'd possessed since the day of his birth. Since then, he'd done next to nothing to develop it. He was sensitive enough to qualify as a Singer without effort. In that regard, he and Presnell were much alike.

Because of the unique circumstances, he'd never developed the obsession and fascination with the Song of the Engines so many Singers did. His gift, and the Song itself, were nothing more than a means to the end.

His desires were every bit as pragmatic. He wanted to be comfortable. He wanted to survive, and he wanted to see his city do the same. The recent birth of twins added another desire, which was to establish a future in which his children would enjoy the same quality of life he'd enjoyed, if not a better one.

To those ends, he saw the Seer as a necessary ally in

the chaos to come. Of all Nightkeep's leadership, he was perhaps the only one who offered the Seer proper respect.

Still, the Seer was far from popular among the Singers, especially now, and to keep his position, Dougan pressed harder than he would have in private. "Surely by now you've sensed the happenings around Firestone."

One benefit of the long walk was that the Seer had enjoyed plenty of time to spin his story properly. He bowed, pretending obsequiousness. "I have, sir. The work of Kaya, no doubt, attempting to draw the nuddu away from Underhill. Perhaps also preparation to strike at Nightkeep. Surely by now, word of her sentence has reached her."

The looks around the table told the Seer the other Singers had already guessed much the same.

"Was it successful?" Dougan asked.

The question carried a weight far beyond the immediate moment. These fools knew so little about the nuddu, they certainly wondered if perhaps a single city could be sacrificed to distract the creatures from the others.

Let them think whatever they want. "I'm unsure. I was listening to the competing songs when I was summoned, and I had to break the connection."

Several of the Singers shifted in their seats. The Seer spoke as if the breaking of the connection was an unfortunate necessity, but few of the assembly missed his jab at the head Singer. They could stew on that the next time they saw fit to disturb him.

Dougan was forced to acquiesce. "I apologize for having to summon you on such short notice, but we felt the situation justified the disruption to your efforts. Do you think Firestone's efforts succeeded?"

The Seer pretended to debate the answer, then said, "I

do. Such is the strength of Firestone's Engine, it seems improbable the nuddu would ignore it."

That sent them into a tizzy. He stood before them and let their discussion wash over him. The room fell into a disarray that matched his state as three different arguments fought for primacy. Dougan allowed the chaos longer than he should have, then raised a hand for silence. Like the Seer, he'd said nothing, tracking the various arguments and distilling them to their core problems. He addressed the Seer with the first of these.

"Is this a strategy that could be duplicated by other cities?"

The temptation to laugh out loud struck again, and again he reined in his impulse. That they would ask him, the man who'd authored the nuddu's escape and their initial targets, how to best protect themselves was an irony so rich he wouldn't need dessert for a week. He savored the moment while he pretended to think. "I believe so. There is a question of whether the nuddu can learn, which I don't know. Our safest bet remains mastery of the shadow song, but we would be fools not to investigate the idea further."

Dougan didn't realize he was being led around by the nose, so perfectly did the Seer's answer lead into his next question. "Does it require a power equivalent to Kaya's?"

"Once again, I'm not sure, and I think you all, as Singers, would know better than me. All I can say is I've never sensed an Engine do anything similar, which to my mind implies it is a gift only she can bring."

His answers inspired another round of discussion, which both he and Dougan once again endured in silence. Once the greater part of the arguments had faded, Dougan set the matter before the Singers in a decisive manner. "I don't know how long Veylan plans to wait before journeying to Firestone and executing Kaya. Does this change our plans at all?"

Half the table argued that Kaya needed to be captured and interrogated. The other half wanted her head on a stake.

The Seer leaned back, rubbed his temples, and sighed. He feared this would take a while, and it was all meaningless. Even if they decided to reverse course, Veylan and Parnell would execute Kaya before word reached them.

He could have told them the strategy wouldn't work, but word about the nuddu pursuing Firestone would soon reach their ears. Their decision to execute Kaya would divide them, though, which served his purposes well. Any division could be exploited with time and careful consideration. If he had to endure this meeting as the cost of that division, it was a price he would gladly pay.

He couldn't track the shadow song as closely without the shrine, but he could still hear it, and so the arguments of the Singers faded into the background as he listened and waited. The nuddu would sing with joy as they devoured the Engines in both Firestone and Underhill, and he would know his ultimate victory was complete.

22

Kaya watched the nuddu's advance with eyes born to see light and dark and senses that listened to both the Song of the Engine and the shadow song, and Firestone was close enough no detail could escape her notice. Radyn had already surrendered the fight, his back to the monster as he took his first step toward Tanwen.

The shadow song vibrated like a string tied between two posts and plucked. One endpoint curled around what passed as the nuddu's spirits, and she followed the darkness long enough to locate the source, that same infinite blackness from the bog. It was on the move now, adjacent to a Song that was all too familiar.

"Radyn, wait a moment," she said.

He paused and glanced back. The nuddu took one lumbering step toward Underhill, then stopped. They didn't twist as a human would have. Instead, their back legs lifted and stretched out at nearly right angles from the creatures' torsos, the shadows within twisting and expanding to accommodate the new shape. The leading leg, now left behind, retreated, the whole leg sucked back into the torso. It emerged pointing right at Firestone.

Kaya suppressed the shudder that ran through her body. Every other creature, no matter how vile, at least had the decency to maintain a solid shape. The amorphous nature of the nuddu unsettled her, for what violence could defeat what amounted to a deadly cloud? The nuddu grew larger as its long strides devoured the distance between it and Firestone.

Radyn once again stood by her side, his retreat ended prematurely by the success of their strategy. "They're gaining fast. How soon before we stop rising and start running?"

Kaya looked over the edge. The bottom tip of Firestone was still low enough to crash into the peaks of the highest of the surrounding hills, but Radyn's judgment was true. The sheer mass of cities meant they couldn't accelerate quickly, even with the incredible power of the Engines. If they didn't start running soon, the nuddu's greater speed would overtake them. All the legends agreed on one fact: as soon as a nuddu made contact, the city's future would be measured in minutes.

She joined the Singers down below, weaving her song among theirs without their permission. Shock ran through the group, but she twisted their song and issued new commands to the Engine. She hated such crude measures, but there was no time for gentler methods. Firestone lurched as the Engine strained, but it started moving laterally. Kaya pointed them southwest, toward the lowest of the surrounding hills. The city both rose and traveled. Firestone might not escape the hills unharmed, but damage to the lower levels could be withstood, while the grip of a nuddu could not. Certain the Singers understood and respected her intent, she broke away from their song and turned her full attention to the nuddu, which still closed the distance quickly.

"This seemed like a much better idea when the nuddu wasn't so close," Radyn said.

Kaya didn't respond. She tilted her head to the side, as though studying the nuddu from a new angle would lead to a greater understanding. She frowned and squinted.

"What?" Radyn asked.

"Those nuddu are being controlled," Kaya said.

"How?"

"By the Seer, I would guess. Or one of the shadow warriors we stumbled upon in the bog. The source of the shadow I felt in the bog is on Nightkeep now. The nuddu are following its commands. That's why they turned. The Seer wants Firestone dead."

"He's behind all this?"

"Or at least a big part."

Radyn cursed. "No way to get to him on Nightkeep, though. We don't have nearly enough Manirah to launch a successful attack, and with Nightkeep allied with many of the other cities against you, we won't find any help either, if anyone even believes us."

Kaya grimaced. She still hated what she'd done to Nightkeep. She'd imagined the scene a hundred times since then, and never once stumbled upon a better answer. The drop had been the only way to protect Firestone and Underhill. She'd never guessed it would doom them in the eyes of others.

Radyn's comments bounced around in her skull, something about them tickling at her thoughts. She could feel the idea as a seed, but it refused to grow.

He interrupted her with another curse just as she thought she'd coaxed it out of the ground. "Doesn't matter anyway. Veylan is here. A lot earlier than I expected."

The warmth drained from her face. Despite knowing the fate of her spirit, she hadn't had time to face the dire reality of her sentence. Healing Firestone and protecting Underhill had distracted her. Only now, when she saw the silhouette of the dragon bearing her executioner, did the proximity of her death strike fear into her bones.

Icy hands gripped her heart, and her knees almost gave out. Her breath came in short, ragged gasps, and she would have lost her balance if Radyn hadn't noticed her distress and steadied her. They watched the approaching dragon, and in that shadow, Kaya saw not just her death, but the end of the Song.

Father would have accused her of being dramatic, but she didn't think so. For generations, the forces of shadow had been contained, but the Seer had found a way to break the chains that had held them. There were dozens, if not hundreds, of Singers who might someday contest the shadow, but they were blinded by the instructions handed down to them by their masters. They would need to relearn, and such learning took more time than they had. Without her to guide their way, it would be even longer. Too long, considering the strides the Seer made every day.

She gripped Radyn's arm. "Wait."

He looked at her, a question in his expression.

"You said we couldn't reach the Seer on Nightkeep, but that's not true."

"What do you mean?"

Kaya's thoughts began to race, tumbling one after the other. "You and I can invade Nightkeep through Firestone's Engine."

Radyn's face paled. "I can't travel between the Engines like you can."

"You can. You've joined me when I traveled using my spirit, and having the body follow isn't much harder. We can show up inside Nightkeep's Engine room, then make our way to the Seer."

"You make it sound easy. They'll have guards everywhere, and our arrival will stir up a fuss."

"I know Nightkeep's schedule. At least, I did when I was younger. There are always two or three Singers on duty at a minimum, but the only time there's more than that is if they're making course changes or something special comes up. Chances are good there will only be a few Singers close to the Engine room, and probably no more than a few guards at the door. If we can fight our way through them and into the city without raising an alarm, we should be free. You're not dressed as a Sword, and I'm not dressed as a Singer, so neither of us will attract any attention once we're there. The Singers might notice our arrival, but I'm not so sure that they will. My last pass through the Engines didn't alert anyone."

Radyn gripped her arm to slow the outpouring of thoughts. His eyes flicked back and forth as he imagined the scenario she described, and he swallowed hard, because he'd realized what she said could be done.

She spoke more slowly. "We kill the Seer, capture the source of the shadow, and put an end to all this."

"And after?" Radyn asked.

"If we can, we make it back to the Engine and escape back here to Firestone."

"That doesn't save your life. Veylan will be here."

Her knees trembled and threatened to collapse again, but she feigned nonchalance. "I was sentenced to die regardless. At least this way, I can save everyone else."

His expression told her that he'd seen through her deception, but he said nothing.

"It's up to you. One way or the other, they'll hunt me

down until I'm dead. You still have a chance at a more normal life. Aria and your child are waiting for you."

She couldn't say whether she wanted him to stay or go, but when he gave a single curt nod, relief passed through her. She hated to risk his life alongside hers, but so long as he was near, she could face the end with her head held high.

They hurried back to the stairs that would lead them into the bowels of Firestone. Before they left the surface for the last time, Kaya paused. Veylan's dragon grew larger by the moment, but this might very well be her last time under an open sky. She closed her eyes and turned her face to the sun, its warmth strong against her cheeks. One long breath imprinted the feeling in her memory.

She wiped a tear out of the corner of her eye, then followed Radyn as he made his way toward the Engine room.

———

Two levels down, all of Firestone tilted and shuddered. The sudden shift threw Kaya against a wall, bruising her shoulder as flesh met Makers' steel. She grimaced and reached for the Song, but Firestone's Engine was constant and strong.

Radyn realized the cause before her. "I think we just collided with one of the hills."

Firestone groaned as it righted itself, and Kaya nodded, her heart pounding hard from the surprise. "Right." She tried to lighten the mood. "Probably good we weren't on the observation deck, then."

Radyn made a half-grunt, half-snort that passed as a laugh. "Probably."

When they reached the Engine room, they found the

Singers loitering in the hallway outside. They looked tired but pleased with their efforts. Orenil raised his gaze as they came running down the hallway. He found the strength for a weak smile. "How close are the nuddu?"

"Close. How are you?"

Orenil shrugged. "I feel worn thin. I've never come close to singing this much in a day. Our course is steady, though. Once we've reached a slightly safer altitude, we'll correct one last time and hope to outrun the nuddu. Just need to take a bit of a break first."

"Veylan is here," Kaya announced.

The Singer's eyes narrowed. "So soon? What are you going to do?"

"I'm going to see if I can strike a blow against the shadow song. Radyn will help. I need the Engine, but probably not more than a few moments."

Orenil gestured to the open door. "Be my guest."

"Thank you. Don't do anything foolish with Veylan. There's no need to risk yourself on my account."

Orenil's eyes narrowed as he prepared to object, but Kaya silenced him with a kiss. She let her lips linger against his, tasting the dried sweat of his prolonged efforts. She broke away before her will failed her and marched toward the open Engine room, Radyn a step behind her.

Once inside, Radyn closed the door and sealed it. He lit his maniblade and thrust it into the door, cutting through the bolt between the lock and frame so that if someone tried to unseal the door, the heavy bolt would remain in place. It wouldn't delay anyone with a maniblade long, but every moment might matter.

Kaya went straight to the Engine and embraced the Song. It slipped from her grasp on her first attempt, her mind in too many places at once. She tried again, but once more her focus failed her. She thought of Orenil, exhausted but steadfast; of Veylan, honor-bound and afraid; and of her father, broken and consumed by shadow.

Radyn's hand on her shoulder steadied her, and her gaze met his. "Be here now. It's all that has ever mattered."

The words drove the distracting thoughts from her head like a diligent shepherd herding stray sheep. "Thanks."

Kaya joined her spirit to the Song. Only once had she traveled physically between the Engines, and that moment had been driven more by the Song than by her conscious choice. Despite the harrowing terror of that moment, her body and spirit retained the memory of that shifting.

Her song began as little more than a whisper, like a child humming a nursery rhyme to themselves to fall asleep at night. It grew in power, encompassing both her and Radyn in its grasp. Her body began to feel like a mirage, insubstantial before the Song. She reached out and took Radyn's hand, then looked to him for confirmation. She wanted to give him one last chance to make a different choice.

A metallic thudding sound came from the door. Veylan's face was pressed up against the window as he yelled. He pounded on the door with the hilt of his maniblade again.

Radyn squeezed her hand. With her free hand, she reached out and touched the Engine, and the world fell away.

23

Radyn was no Singer, but he'd spent most of his life in close contact with the Song of the Engines. He was no stranger to the beauty and power held within the mighty constructions, reflected in life throughout the world. He'd even followed Kaya's spirit as it traveled deeper into the Song than he would have ever dared.

None of what he'd experienced before prepared him for the transition between the Engines. His sense of self, so closely tied to the physical boundaries of his body, dissolved against the powerful currents of the Song. His spirit was borne upon waves of power that crested with blinding ferocity, leaving him feeling like a wounded minnow caught in the current of a roaring rapid.

The Song battered him and threatened to tear him apart, shredding his spirit and scattering the scraps across the continent. There was nothing physical for him to grasp onto, no anchor he could use to steady mind or spirit. He sensed Kaya surrounding him, protecting him from a realm not meant for human spirits to traverse.

They emerged on a platform standing next to an

Engine, and for a brief, sickening moment, Radyn feared Kaya's efforts had been for naught, that the powers attacking him had been nothing more than the normal outpourings of the Song when one was foolish enough to touch an Engine. Except Veylan's face wasn't pressed up against this window, and the door to the Engine room lacked the scar Radyn had so recently inflicted upon Firestone's door.

His hand went to his maniblade and he began to connect with his shards, but Kaya's hand upon his arm arrested the instinct. "Use your maniblade if you must, but try not to connect to your other shards. They don't know we're here yet."

Radyn followed Kaya's advice. He grabbed his maniblade and stepped toward the door, only to have the whole world spin around him. He stumbled and caught himself on the railing.

"Take a moment," Kaya advised. "I think we earned it."

Radyn sagged against the railing as spirit and body aligned once again. As Kaya had predicted, there were no Singers in the room, and he said a silent thanks to whatever fates oversaw the doings of madmen. He might have been able to fight, but he had no desire to test himself. "I can't believe that worked."

He took some small comfort in seeing that Kaya suffered much as he did. She was leaning against an opposite railing. "One of the major failings of the Singers' teachings is that spirit and flesh are separate entities. They aren't one and the same, but they're far more entwined than the Singers believe. Swords and Daggers, I think, understand the reality a bit more intuitively, since you take the Song into your bodies to strengthen them."

Kaya tossed out the knowledge as though it meant

nothing, a throw-away fact of little importance. Radyn stared. "Why don't Singers know?"

"Because their task is to sing, to manipulate the Engines using their spirits. Swords and Daggers are dancing with the Song instead of commanding it. The easiest way to sing is to think of the Song as something separate."

Radyn pushed himself off the railing. They had a chance to stop shadow here, but Kaya needed to live. What she knew was too important. He couldn't weigh that against the fate of Firestone, but there had to be a way that both Firestone and Kaya survived. He only had to find it. "You could travel between any two Engines, right?"

Kaya glanced up at Nightkeep's Engine. "I think so, why?"

"When we return here, we should think about traveling somewhere else."

Kaya's expression darkened. "We'll worry about that when the time comes. That's too big a decision to make in a hurry."

She marched toward the door before he could respond, and he had no choice but to follow. She opened the door, much to the surprise of the two Singers sitting at a table in the room just beyond. One was an elderly woman, her gray hair turning to a white that would match her Singer's robes. The other was a woman who looked young enough to be the first Singer's granddaughter. Both had eyes almost as wide as the teacups that sat before them.

Radyn spun the hilt of his maniblade in his hand and struck the younger woman with the bottom. Her eyes rolled up in her head and she collapsed against the table. He took a step and wrapped his arm around the older woman's neck, applying pressure. The woman struggled for a moment, stronger than she appeared.

"Sorry about this, ma'am," Radyn said.

She reached for his eyes, but he kept his head out of reach, and soon her body went limp. He held on a moment longer to ensure she was unconscious, then let her go, supporting her head until she was resting over the table. At the briefest of glances, it might look like they were sleeping, but even that would draw attention. Radyn settled for not having killed them.

The door on the other end of the antechamber opened, the guards on duty drawn in by the sounds of the scuffle. Radyn leaped at them, waking his maniblade as he spun the hilt again in his hand. The first guard collapsed as the tip of the maniblade went through his face, and the second as Radyn cut down and across.

The markings on their uniforms were of a senior Sword and a senior Dagger. He'd been fortunate to catch them by surprise. Had they any chance to fight back, he would have needed the aid of his shards.

Kaya seemed to have barely noticed the fights. Her eyes were unfocused, following threads of shadow and Song through the foreign city. When her eyes returned to focus, she said, "Hide your maniblade. We should be safe, and I have a rough idea where the source of the shadow is."

Radyn stuffed the hilt near the small of his back, held in place by his belt. He lifted the back of his tunic and covered the hilt with it. He ensured he could draw the hilt if necessary, then let the tunic drop over the hilt again. His draw would be slower, but that was the price of concealment. Kaya assured him no one would notice the weapon, and they left the area surrounding the Engine room.

He'd never been on Nightkeep, and the schism between his expectations and reality jarred him. Nightkeep warriors and Singers who'd attacked Firestone and forced Elora to sacrifice her life. They were villains and scoundrels, and when he bothered to think about them, he imagined them all training to conquer Firestone.

Instead of a militant culture focused on conquest, Nightkeep greeted him with scenes that wouldn't be out of place in either Firestone or Underhill. Families waited in line for food outside a kitchen, the parents talking while the children ran underfoot. Laborers carrying baskets of supplies hurried from the surface to the crafting areas on the lower levels. In one hallway, a couple of youths stole kisses and eager embraces from one another.

Radyn and Kaya attracted some notice, being new to the neighborhood, but they walked at an easy pace, greeted those who greeted them, and bowed as Shields on patrol passed by. Nightkeep was too large for the citizens to all know one another, so their passage drew less attention than it would have in a smaller city.

Radyn almost froze when they passed a Nightkeep Dagger, but the young man paid them no attention. The Dagger might know Radyn's name, but they didn't know his face, and they certainly didn't expect him to be wandering their halls. Once the Dagger was out of sight, Radyn's estimations of their chances rose considerably.

His palm itched, longing to hold the maniblade in hand. It wouldn't be so easy when they reached the Seer's hiding place.

After a while of walking, he asked, "Are you sure you know where you're going?" He'd expected them to travel to the lowest levels of the city, someplace away from the hustle and bustle of daily life, a place where the Seer could hide both himself and his prize. Instead, they climbed ever higher and away from the Engine room. They were already a considerable distance from where they'd started.

"I'm sure. It feels as though the source is near the edge of the city."

He'd also forgotten how large Nightkeep was. By the time Kaya finally slowed, it felt as though they'd walked across all of Firestone twice. She came to an intersection and peered around the corner. "I don't see any guards outside, but I can sense presences within the room."

"Any idea how many?" Radyn asked.

"No. More than two, but the strength of the source is making it difficult for me to sense."

Radyn could hardly fault her. He could sense the dark taint of the shadow song through his shards, even though he wasn't fully connected to them. Her experience must be sickening. "Any suggestions?"

"Only to be aware that when you connect with your shards, you'll likely experience a moment of disorientation. Connect before you need to, but not too long before, because they'll sense you in there the moment you do."

Radyn raised an eyebrow and received a shrug.

"I know; still, it's the best advice I have."

Kaya led him into the hallway and to the proper door, though this close to the source of the shadow, Radyn could have guessed himself. Unnatural power oozed from the door like a stain spreading through the hall. Kaya nodded to tell him she was ready.

Radyn fell back on his years of training and experience. He held the hilt of his maniblade as Elora had taught him and examined the door that stood in his way. It looked no different from any other residential door, made of a sheet of Makers' metal about the width of his thumb. One bolt above the doorknob served as the locking mechanism, and a brief study of the seam between the door and the frame revealed no other locks. He stepped back and connected with all his shards.

The heightened sensitivity that came as a result of the connection brought him closer to the Song, but also inundated him with the filthy powers leaking from the room. His stomach twisted as though it had been poisoned, and if he'd been digesting a meal, he was nearly certain he would have thrown up. He held tight to the Song and the moment passed. He lit his maniblade and swiped it down the line where the door met the frame, cutting cleanly through the bolt locking the door shut. A strong kick to the door flung it open, and he leaped inside.

He only had time for a glance. As Kaya had cautioned, his connection with the shards had warned the guards inside, and they were already moving to defend the room as the door opened.

The inside of the room was startling in its mundanity. The door opened into a short hallway that ran for about four paces, and then the wall on the left ended as the hallway became a living room. Radyn's apartment in Underhill was a nearly identical design. He sprinted down the hallway to avoid getting trapped in a narrow space, then met the first of the guards, a small man with shifty eyes.

Twin blades of shadow appeared in the man's hands, and Radyn cursed his luck. He made a hurried cut, hoping to end the duel before the man set himself, but the Seer's disciple held off the attack with one blade and lashed out with his second, nearly as fast as Radyn. The Song rose in Radyn's chest, filling his limbs with fresh strength. He twisted and applied more pressure to the maniblade, forcing the guard to break off his attack and burn his strength to keep the glowing blue blade away from his neck.

Radyn roared and flexed, and his Song-enhanced strength forced the smaller guard back. He pressed his advantage, clearing the hallway so Kaya could enter the room. She held a glowing blade in her hand, but if all the guards were as strong as the one Radyn fought, it wouldn't protect her for long.

He broke away from the first guard as a second joined the fight from the study the hallway wall had hidden from view as Radyn entered. He held a long black blade in his hand, and he attacked with the same technique they taught Shields. Radyn blocked the cut and tried to respond, but the first guard angled in and cut at his wrist. Avoiding the cut wasn't hard, but it prevented Radyn from seizing the upper hand.

Two other figures were emerging from one of the bedrooms, the same room where the shadow was strongest. Their dark robes marked them as visitors from the tribes below, but Radyn didn't have an opportunity to note any further details as two warriors with three shadow weapons pressed their perceived advantage.

Thought fell away as instinct ruled. The blue light of the Song made manifest in his blade fought against the darkness of the shadow song. Blades crossed and clashed, slid off one another and missed completely as the warriors sought any deadly openings. The smaller man with the twin daggers was the worst of the two. He lacked any formal training, but his reflexes must have been preternaturally quick even before he embraced the shadow song, for Radyn couldn't sneak his blade past those twin daggers no matter what he tried.

Nor did he have the time. The shadow warriors from the surface had pounced on Kaya like hungry cats on a mouse. She at least had the good sense to retreat, knowing she was outclassed.

Radyn kicked at the smaller disciple's knee,

unbalancing the disciple for a moment but earning a fresh scar across his thigh in exchange.

The price was more than worth it. At the moment the Shield-trained disciple lost his ally, Radyn fell on him with all the speed his shards granted him. The disciple blocked the first of Radyn's many cuts, but the rest brought him down, his arteries pumping blood like a fountain across the ceiling.

The smaller man charged, sweeping Radyn's maniblade out of the way with one of his daggers. Radyn resisted for a fraction of a heartbeat, then let the maniblade sleep. The disciple twisted as the expected resistance vanished, but by the time he regained his balance, Radyn had lit his maniblade again, and the Seer's disciple helpfully impaled himself on the weapon. Radyn heaved the maniblade out, intent on causing as much damage as he could. The disciple fell to his knees and Radyn cut one last time, both to end the man's suffering and ensure he was out of the fight.

He reached Kaya a moment before she found herself impaled on a shadowy spear. He knocked it aside and joined the fight, driving the shadow warriors back. Little of them was visible. They wore their black robes, but also wrapped the fabric around their heads, leaving nothing but their eyes visible. The loose dark clothing made it difficult to track all their movements.

"Get to the source!" he said.

Kaya nodded and ran toward the bedroom. The smaller of the shadow warriors tried to pursue, but found their path blocked by the glowing blue of Radyn's maniblade. They skidded to a stop, and Radyn shifted so he stood between the two warriors and the source. So long as he kept Kaya safe and gave her the time needed to destroy the source, they could leave the Seer's room with the victory.

Both shadow warriors fell upon him. One seemed best with the dark equivalent of a maniblade, while the other preferred a spear that seemed to writhe with shadowy tendrils of smoke. Radyn was pressed hard, the skills of the shadow warriors nearly comparable to his own. His blade met shadow and was turned away. If he tried to break the guard of one, the other struck into the opening. Shadow cut into his arms and chest, the darkness searching for a hook into his flesh.

Kaya called to him from the room. "There's a problem here. I'll need you."

Radyn risked a glance back, but she'd already retreated into the bedroom. He swore, then swore again as the smaller warrior's spear scratched a new line across his cheek.

That had been a mistake, a lunge that brought the shadow warrior too close. He delivered a punch to their midsection that folded them in half, then twisted to keep the shadow warrior between him and the dark blade that sought his life. He shoved the folded-over warrior at the one with the sword, and they scrambled out of the way.

Radyn followed with his maniblade. The second warrior cried out, and though Radyn didn't speak the language, he heard the agony in the words. His glowing blue blade cut the cry short, and the young man fell, limbs tangling with the second warrior, who still fought to recover their breath.

"Radyn!"

He ran into the bedroom. "What?"

Kaya pointed to what appeared to be a nondescript chest at the foot of the bed. It was bolted to the floor. "What's the problem? Just cut it open."

"I can't. There's a web of shadow around it. If you give me enough time, I could probably work my way through it, but it's way more time than we have. You'd be fighting off all of Nightkeep before I finished."

Radyn cursed. "Stand back."

He closed his eyes and embraced the Song coursing through his veins. He dove deep, pushing the limits of what his body could handle. Light flooded bone, muscle, and sinew, and with a mighty yell, he raised his maniblade. The glow from the weapon lit the room like a dozen lanterns, banishing shadow from every corner of the room. He brought the blade down, and Song and shadow met upon the surface of the chest.

Radyn's spirit trembled as forces far beyond him tore through his body. The Song burned away all the shadow it fought, but this close to the source, shadow strengthened itself with reinforcements that threatened to overwhelm the Song. Radyn was less a combatant and more an observer, the conduit for the Song to travel through. Engines across the continent dimmed as they met their enemy in direct battle. The Song flowed through him, through the hilt of his maniblade, and into the web.

The battle remained even until the moment it wasn't, and then shadow unravelled as though it had never existed. Caught off guard by the sudden lack of resistance, Radyn stumbled forward and cut through the side of the chest. He recovered quickly and sliced his blade through the lock and the hinges, opening the chest completely.

"All yours," he said.

A shadow moved in the doorway, and Radyn barely lifted his maniblade in time to keep the dark spear writhing in shadow from piercing Kaya's back. The spear vanished as soon as it missed, only to reappear in the hands of its master. Radyn moved to strike, then froze.

The dark wrappings that had protected the warrior's face had fallen, possibly torn off as she fought for breath in the other room.

By the gate, though, she was young. She wasn't more than a girl, and he couldn't look at her without thinking of his unborn child growing happily in Aria's belly.

He couldn't make the cut.

A fire burned in her dark eyes, though, and she didn't suffer the same dilemma. She lashed out at him with her spear as he stood there, unable to move.

24

The Seer's body shivered as the Song came in contact with the defensive wards he'd painstakingly established around the chest that guarded the shrine. His eyes went wide. The debate around the Singers' chambers was monotonous and meaningless, and he sat, forgotten but not dismissed, in his chair. He'd been listening to the plucked strings of the shadow song, but his attention had been on a chase far away as Firestone desperately strove to escape the approaching nuddu.

The warning sound of the wards being breached boomed through his bones, and he clutched at his chest as though he'd been kicked by a horse. Such force! Far greater than any single warrior should have been able to bring to bear.

The Singers were slow to notice his distress, but as they did, conversation around the room ground to a halt. "What's wrong?" Dougan asked.

He needed a moment to catch his breath, but then he wheezed, "We're under attack."

His claim was met with blank, skeptical stares. He

couldn't even blame them this time. The attack had caught him by equal surprise, and if not for the flames of distress building in his bones and stomach, reverberating through his very being, he would have doubted it, too. They were in Nightkeep, the safest, most defended city of them all, and there'd been no warning of an incoming attack.

In hindsight, though, they'd been terribly vulnerable all along.

"Are you certain you're feeling well?" Dougan asked.

"It's Kaya and Radyn. They're in my quarters, attacking the shrine."

One of the other Singers scoffed. "That's impossible. At the beginning of this meeting, you told us they were on Firestone. You were quite certain, as I recall."

The Seer clutched at his chest as the attack on the primal song redoubled. "You all know that Kaya learned how to travel through the Engines. My guess is that she brought Radyn with her. Maybe more, but those two, for sure."

Dougan finally began to take him seriously. "They're attacking us through the Engine room?"

The Seer was already on his feet, sweat beading down his brow. This room was too small, too warm. The wards on the shrine wouldn't last. Did they plan to steal it? Could Kaya turn it to her command?

He didn't think so, but who was he to say? She'd been surprising him nearly as long as he'd kept his eye on her. Anything was possible. He envisioned all his plans and efforts unravelling for good and his knees, not strong at the best of times, almost gave out.

He made it to the door before Dougan stopped him. "Just where do you think you're going?"

"I'll save the shrine. You should send some Swords to my room to help. Meanwhile, order the rest of the available Manirah to the Engine room. It's their only escape."

Dougan stood before the door, arm in front of the Seer, while he considered. After thinking three times as long as necessary, he finally agreed. "I'm not sure that I believe you, but there's no way for them to escape from the surface, so we'll send everyone we can command to the Engine room."

The Seer pushed to escape, but Dougan's arm was firm. "They are not to be harmed."

The Seer froze, certain he'd misheard. "What?"

"At the very least, we need to speak with Kaya. If she can help protect Nightkeep from the nuddu, it's worth the risk. We don't think she'll bring us down. If she wanted to, she would have already."

Too late, the Seer realized his jaw was hanging open. He hadn't paid much attention to the discussion, but it seemed to have changed Dougan's mind on Kaya's fate. The Seer cursed silently. Kaya couldn't be captured alive. If she'd come here, she knew enough to unravel every lie the Seer had wrapped himself in, and Nightkeep would know the truth.

He came close to forming a shadow blade and swiping it across Dougan's throat, but he couldn't afford to lose Nightkeep. Not quite yet.

He forced himself to nod, to pretend like his world wasn't falling apart. "Of course. If I come across them first, I'll do everything possible to capture them. Her knowledge is too valuable to waste, especially now that she's among us." The words tasted like bile on his tongue.

The Master of the Song let the Seer pass. Some of his strength had returned as the wards around the chest had been breached, and maintaining them no longer drew on his reserves. He hurried as fast as his weak knees could carry him. The shrine was unprotected. Whether Kaya could hurt the shrine was an open question, but he wasn't in the mood to gamble. He had to get back to his place before Kaya had too much time alone with the shrine, and he had to reach them first.

Kaya and Radyn needed to die before they fell into Nightkeep's merciful clutches.

25

Kaya paid little attention to the commotion behind her. Radyn guarded her back, which meant that she had nothing to fear. He wouldn't let any warrior harm her with a weapon of bound shadow.

That did nothing to protect her from the dark cube that sat before her. The challenge would be hers alone to face, and she couldn't guess if her mastery of the Song was strong enough to overcome the overwhelming power emanating from the object. She probed at the cube with her senses, avoiding contact until there was no other choice.

As near as she could tell, the cube was perfect in its construction, each face perfectly smooth, each edge and vertex sharp enough to slice easily through unwary flesh. The various resemblances to an Engine were too great to be coincidence. She'd been referring to the cube as the source, but a closer examination revealed that it was no more the source of shadow than the city Engines were the source of the Song. The Song lived and breathed within the Engines, and they were containers and passages for the

Song, but the Song didn't originate within them. Likewise, shadow grew and was strengthened within the cube, but its origin was deeper yet.

If they could find the origin, perhaps they'd finally free their world from the curse of the shadow.

Probing the cube with her spiritual senses revealed little up close she hadn't sensed from a distance. The strands of shadow that spread across the continent were connected to this cube. Destroy it, and the Seer's control over the nuddu should fade as well. The interior of the cube was too well guarded, though, for her senses to dive any deeper.

Kaya returned to her physical senses and heard the sounds of struggle growing close. Radyn was hard-pressed, but she didn't turn her head. Instead, she formed a small dagger of glowing blue light, the Song made manifest in the palm of her hand. She took one deep breath to steady herself, then plunged the blade into the cube.

The cube swallowed the light whole, her maniblade sinking into the cube as though it were soft flesh. Though lost to sight, she still sensed the maniblade complete and unharmed, as though the cube was nothing more than an illusion.

It struck back with visceral force less than a heartbeat later, its temporary retreat from the light only a tactical maneuver to allow it to mass its strength for the counterattack. Shadow shot hundreds, if not thousands, of tiny tendrils of power into her maniblade. The Song of the Engines burned copious amounts away, but the quantity was such that shadow gained a desperate foothold anyway. Burning incredible amounts of itself as sacrifice, it shot up the maniblade and straight into her spirit.

The world vanished as shadow enveloped her soul.

Visions unspooled before her spiritual sight. Cities, falling from the sky, intent on one last devastating act before they lost all say in this world's future. They were mountains falling, an almost impossible amount of mass accelerated to bone-shattering speeds as they burned away their altitude. Anyone still alive inside would be pressed up against the ceilings, using the last air in their lungs to scream for help that would never come.

When the stone of the city collided with the land, everything died. The livestock and humans in the city never had a chance. They were squished like bugs by the unbelievable forces acting upon them, and those that survived the moment of impact were doomed to be crushed by countless tons of steel and stone as the city came apart.

Those that died were the lucky ones, for any who survived were trapped with no way out and no rescue coming. The only humans who remained were pledged to shadow, and no help would arrive. Their end was slow and merciless, and Kaya tried to turn away, but shadow's grip over her vision was absolute.

The falling cities did more than commit suicide. The blasts from the impacts leveled the lands for miles around each site, turning rich and verdant grasslands, forests, and streams into barren, lifeless wastelands. Anything too close to the falling cities was simply gone, torn into bits too small for the eye to see. Farther out were piles of dead animals, bones broken as they were picked up by the force of the impact and tossed about. Blood, bone, and shattered trees collected in a depression filling slowly with water, a grisly stew no survivor dared near. Clouds of dust rose high into the sky, blotting out the sun for years to come.

Kaya's spirit grieved the sights, but if shadow had hoped to drive her to despair, it had failed. She found her voice, which echoed in the dark spaces shadow surrounded her with. "You've shown me nothing I haven't already imagined. This is what I would stop, and I will give all I can to prevent this day from arriving."

Shadow didn't respond to her boast. The visions continued to unspool, day turning to night and back to day in the blink of an eye. Those who served shadow perished, and still the future advanced, one relentless day after the other.

Eventually the clouds of dust began to clear. Small grasses began to poke out of the soil, daring the open air and hungry predators for a daily glimpse of the sun. Seeds of trees sprouted, fed by the rich soil created by the fires of that deadly day so long ago. Bugs and worms worked the soil better than any farmer, drawing small predators and birds to the land. Various seeds found their way into the cracks in the stone of the fallen cities, and as soil collected around the stone, blown by the storms that passed through, those seeds, too, began to sprout, bringing life to the mass graveyards.

She couldn't guess how many years had passed since the cities had fallen from the sky, but time healed all wounds. It was as true for the human spirit as it was for the continent humanity had once called home. The world went on, the land went on, and soon, humans were forgotten altogether.

This was what the Seer had seen, then.

"No. I know what you would have me say, for that was his argument as well. I don't believe it, or better yet, I choose not to believe it. The world's flourishing doesn't require humanity's destruction. I believe there can be both."

Shadow struck straight at her spirit, as dark and malevolent as she'd ever felt it, but it found no hold there. It gripped and tried to hold on, but so long as her spirit burned bright, it could do nothing but throw visions at her.

It spent itself at an incredible rate, but to no avail. Shadow was the weaker power. If it met the Song on equal terms, the Song would win, the strength of life greater than the void that sought to swallow it.

So shadow deceived. It sapped the spirits from its victims so they didn't have the strength to fight, and once its claws were planted, it didn't let go. She'd seen too often the results of its efforts. Even the best couldn't hold out hope once shadow had its hooks in. Even Jelrik, for all his strength and wisdom, hadn't been able to fight the despair for long.

She blinked and encountered another vision, one where the cities remained in the sky, but at the cost of the Song's strength. The cities pulled and pulled, thinking not at all of the destruction they left behind. The end wasn't nearly as dramatic as the cities falling. Trees withered, grasses turned brown, and animals lost weight they couldn't afford to surrender, and still, the humans pulled from the Song until there was nothing left.

"You sell us too short," Kaya said. "Your visions show only what may be, not what will be, and I have faith. We've always found the way forward before, and we will this time, too."

Shadow slipped from her spirit. Light burned away the shadow within the cube despite its desperate struggles, and its grip weakened.

Far from defeated, though, shadow sought a different crack in her spirit's armor. Once the crack was found, it dove in.

She blinked to reveal new visions, though these had a different weight to them than the first. Those had been illusions, based only weakly in reality. Here the shadow revealed a causal chain, projecting her immediate future. It presented her choice and understood the impulses of her spirit and mind, revealing the consequences of each decision.

She defeated the cube, then narrowly escaped Nightkeep with Radyn in tow. She returned to Firestone, and there was a fight. Radyn, still disoriented from his travel between the Engines, was no match for Veylan. He died never having seen his child, and Kaya, unable to defend herself against Veylan's maniblade, followed him through the gate a moment later.

No.

She wasn't ready to die. Not when she was so close to understanding the source and purpose of the shadow, and if it was within her power, she refused to be responsible for Radyn's death.

Shadow responded to her spirit's desire, revealing the future she thought she wanted. Once again they narrowly escaped Nightkeep's pursuit, but this time Kaya found the way to another Engine, a city far to the north. When she didn't return to Firestone, her father, who was the Singer who accompanied Veylan, demanded the justice Veylan had threatened. Tied tight by the bonds of honor, Veylan ordered Firestone's Singers to raise Firestone high into the sky and position it straight over Underhill. Orenil resisted and lost his life in the effort. Eventually the deed was done and the Singers killed. Kaya's father put Firestone's Engine to sleep just before escaping on Veylan's dragon. The city fell onto Underhill, leaving no survivors among either the soulkeepers or Firestone's citizenry. Radyn fell into a bleak depression, making him an easy target for shadow to corrupt, and Kaya was eventually forced to submit to Nightkeep's justice.

Panic bubbled up through her spirit. Every attempt to seal it away failed, and so she sought a different path.

Shadow sensed her distress and was all too eager to

reveal the consequences of each choice. She tried hiding on Nightkeep and finding her way off. She tried returning Radyn to Firestone and then escaping alone. Her decisions grew more desperate. She crashed one of Nightkeep's cities. She crashed them all.

No more.

Shadow wasn't done, sensing the despair it had successfully planted in her spirit, but resolution sealed the cracks it had exploited. One set of paths remained, and though it was tempting to allow shadow to predict them, she feared the consequences.

That was the point of hope, after all. Where certainty existed, there was no need for hope, for knowledge reigned supreme. Hope bloomed only in the unknown. More than that, it was a choice. A choice not to surrender, despite everything standing against her. In the dark, surrounded by the shadow of the cube, it was all she had, but it was enough to protect her spirit from any further visions.

The shadow faded, forced to spend all its strength simply to defend itself against the Song that had physically pierced its protection. She pushed her maniblade deeper into the cube, placing all her weight upon the weapon. The shadow fought her for every bit, her strength bleeding away as the shadow leeched it away.

Kaya called upon the Engines.

Nightkeep's massive Engines, some of the largest the Makers had ever created, responded to her call, giving of themselves to rid their homes of the cursed object. Stone and steel groaned as the city tilted from the sudden lack of power, but Kaya's maniblade grew as bright as the sun. A scream was ripped from her throat as she asked her soul for everything it could offer.

Against the aligned strength of her spirit and the Engines, the cube couldn't stand. It fought tooth and nail to survive, spending every bit of itself before one of the dark threads connecting it to something deeper snapped. The material of the cube cracked as the thread broke, and the shadow was stripped of its seemingly endless reinforcement. One last shout, one last push, drove the maniblade through the other side of the cube. It cracked open loudly enough to ring in Kaya's ears.

She let the maniblade vanish as she slumped against the side of the bed. Though the powers hadn't come from within, her body had served as the channel for the Song to flow, and exhaustion stole the fire from her spirit. Her eyes closed.

They opened again as her physical senses returned to primacy. Radyn breathed hard, grunting against what sounded to be a vicious assault. The dull thuds of a maniblade connecting with a shadow sword repeated endlessly, beating nearly as fast as her heart.

She cracked open an eye just in time to see Radyn fall backward, a young girl with a dark blade standing victorious, ready to kill him.

26

Radyn's hesitation only lasted long enough for the girl to strike at him. Despite her youth, she was skilled, and that skill was backed by a remarkable determination. She manipulated the shadow weapons with an ease any Manirah would covet. One moment she would fight with a sword that matched his maniblade; the next she'd have two daggers in hand. If he retreated too far, she switched to a long spear. Once, Radyn raised his maniblade to block a dagger, only for the dagger to disappear the moment before contact and reappear on the back side of his blade, as though it had passed straight through. A quick step back had resulted in nothing worse than a torn tunic, but if he'd been connected to any less of his shards, the resulting cut would have been fatal.

The ice that locked his limbs melted as she attacked, but he couldn't strike back at her. He blocked, dodged, parried, and kept himself between the deadly youth and Kaya, but not once did he attempt to cut her down. The mere thought of doing so slowed his reactions, made it feel like he was pulling a steel sword through water.

The vision of Aria pregnant wouldn't leave him be. It haunted him like a ghost, lingering over his shoulder, judging every action.

Skilled as the girl was, she didn't have the speed to beat him. All he needed was one missed cut, one off-balance moment, and the fight could be his.

She cut at him and he let his maniblade sleep, sliding to the side of the cut instead of blocking, a taste of her own skill reflected upon her. The move caught her by surprise, and her unopposed momentum carried her nearly to the other side of the bedroom. As she passed, she was entirely undefended.

If he'd willed, he could have woken his maniblade as she passed and the weapon would have passed straight through her side. Nothing could have been easier.

Instead, she passed by him unharmed, and he only woke his weapon once she was clear. Her eyes narrowed, as though seeing him in an entirely new light, and then her face twisted in a vicious grin. She crouched, and before she launched herself, Radyn knew he was in for a fight that would push him to his limit.

One he could have avoided. One he could still avoid, if he could find the will. If he could brush the ghost off his shoulder and bear the shame of his actions alone.

The young woman switched to daggers and struck at Radyn with a whirlwind of cuts that approached from every conceivable angle. He blocked what he could and retreated from the rest, ceding ground as fast as a clan being routed. Her wild attacks left her vulnerable to any number of counters, but she had weighed his spirit accurately. There was no way of avoiding her shadow blades, remaining unharmed, and staying between her and Kaya. As soon as Radyn was out of position, she leaped at Kaya.

The Singer didn't notice. She'd driven a maniblade into what looked like a dark cube, and the energies at play dwarfed anything Radyn was capable of manipulating. Radyn jumped at the young woman, who twisted as he attempted to tackle her. Daggers rose in defense, and they punched through his side as he tackled her onto the bed.

The impact jarred the young woman's focus, and her deadly blades vanished before they could carve Radyn's insides into a bloody goo. They landed in a heap, legs and arms tangled. Radyn grunted as fire ripped through the side of his torso, a fierce reminder the young woman had opened a new and unwelcome cut in his flesh. In a moment, he mastered the pain, but the moment was all the small, lithe warrior needed to disentangle herself and form her blades again.

Nightkeep tilted and groaned, and a wave of conflicting powers washed over Radyn and nearly knocked him senseless. Fortunately, the effect was no less pronounced on his opponent, whose eyes rolled up in her head. The sudden disorientation, layered on top of the tilting room, sent the young woman tumbling out of the bed. Radyn, still on his side, rolled like a barrel, grasping for handholds that didn't exist. He rolled off the bed and crashed into the young woman.

Nightkeep righted itself as the woman regained awareness. She formed a dagger and punched at the bottom of Radyn's chin, hoping to drive a wedge of shadow up through his mouth and into his brain. He snapped his head back and let momentum carry him away from her. He rolled over his back and came to his feet, holding his side.

Light exploded from Kaya's maniblade and forced him to close his eyes. The war between the Song and shadow reached its climax, and the shadow winked out as though it had never been more than an illusion. Radyn blinked away the last afterimages of the light in time to see the young woman on her feet. He raised his maniblade to block her daggers, but was too slow to respond to her foot as it came up and kicked him squarely in the chest.

The force of it lifted him off his feet, and there was nothing he could do but wait for the ground to rush up and meet him. He landed hard, and his breath hurried out of him as though it were late for an appointment. The young woman raised her daggers to kill him, then reconsidered where the threat truly lurked. She turned to Kaya, who was currently defenseless after her struggle against the shadow.

He had no way to block the attack. He couldn't get between the girl and Kaya in time.

Radyn rolled to his feet and leaped as the young woman's daggers came down. His maniblade flashed in a sweeping arc, aided by all the shards in his body. Its light was dim compared to what Kaya had just manifested, and it dimmed further as fresh-spilled blood covered the weapon.

Radyn landed for the second time on the bed. A body thumped heavily to the floor, its life stolen. Radyn squeezed his eyes shut and allowed himself a single moment of grief.

Then he stood and helped Kaya to her feet. She rose easily, an expression on her face that startled Radyn into stillness, a radiance he was sure he wasn't just imagining. He blinked and it was gone, though there was an iron certainty behind her gaze that would have caused the Seer to tremble if he'd witnessed it. She shook her head gently, as though emerging from a trance, then ran her gaze over him.

She didn't seem surprised to find the wound bleeding freely at his side. "You're hurt."

"I don't think she cut anything that will be fatal. I only need healing."

She didn't answer, her gaze locked onto something he couldn't see.

"Kaya, is something wrong?" he asked.

For one worried beat of his heart, there was no answer. Breath escaped softly through pursed lips, and then she straightened, and again he swore something within her glowed. He remained connected to his shards and extended his senses toward her, listening for any change in the Song.

She was on fire.

Her strength and ability were no secret, and he sensed no real change in the quantity of her power. Its quality, though, had evolved into something far greater than what it had been when she stepped inside this room. She reminded him of an Engine, crystalline and pure, her Song filled with certain purpose. In fighting the shadow within the source, her spirit had aligned with the Song of the Engines so closely it was difficult to tell them apart.

It boded well for them and terrible for their enemies, and the wound in his side felt like nothing.

Kaya would find a way.

She said, "No. There's nothing wrong. Everything is as it should be."

"Then we should get out of here."

She was once again slow to respond. "I agree. I'll lead the way."

Radyn didn't argue. She'd grown up here and knew the corridors better. "I'll be close behind if anything happens."

"Put your maniblade away."

Radyn obeyed, though his hands wanted nothing more

than to hold Elora's hilt tightly. They left the apartment through the open door and emerged into chaos.

The sight was all too familiar, tearing him from the moment and carrying him years into the past, back to that terrible day all the citizens of Firestone now called the "Little Fall," as though mocking it would erase the terror of those moments and the struggle of the aftermath.

Many of Nightkeep's citizens wandered the halls. One young woman, no older than the girl Radyn had just killed, stood in their way, blood dripping down the side of her face from a gash across her forehead. The blood had sealed one eye closed, and the other stared at nothing, or perhaps the remains of the life she'd once known. Kaya squeezed around her, then hurried on.

Many doors in the hallways were open. In some, families sat together, comforting one another. Wails came from other rooms, both young and old. Radyn stopped outside one from which an infant's cries echoed. He heard no one attempting to soothe the child, and he was walking into the room before Kaya grabbed his wrist and pulled him down the hallway.

"You caused this?" he asked.

She nodded, her pace never slowing. "I wasn't strong enough to fight the shadow on my own. I asked for the Engines to help, and Nightkeep's was only too happy to do so. The effort weakened the Engine, though thankfully only for a few moments."

Had anyone they passed heard, they might have taken issue with Kaya's judgment of the severity of the weakness, but everyone they passed was too lost in their suffering to pay them any attention. They hurried through the hallways like indifferent ghosts, drifting between one scene of suffering and another.

What he noted most, though, was Kaya's tone. She was

a kind spirit who took no pleasure in suffering, yet her voice never wavered as she discussed the aftermath of the battle.

They hurried down a stairwell and came to an intersection where they were stopped by an older man. Beyond a few bruises, he seemed unharmed, but he asked them if they would help him open a nearby door. Radyn was quick to agree, for it could only take a moment, but Kaya once again pulled him forward, leaving the older man confused and angry.

"We could have helped," Radyn said.

Kaya made no answer, her grip on his wrist firm. He shook his hand free. "What happened to you?"

She winced. "There's too much at stake. Please, trust me."

"Kaya, I do. I just want to know what's happening."

She stopped and held a finger to her lips. A door ahead of them opened and a senior Sword and a junior Dagger emerged, maniblades in hand. Radyn tensed, but they didn't turn to look back over their shoulders and spot the intruders. They hurried the other way.

Radyn's eyes narrowed. No matter how good his senses were, he couldn't hear movement on the other side of a door, not with all the other sounds echoing down the hallway.

It couldn't have been a lucky guess, and he didn't believe much in coincidences.

She pulled him forward, and he had no choice but to follow. It was like he was a student in the clan academy again, thrust into a world he wanted to know more about but which was far beyond his understanding. Back then, Elora had been his guide. Today it was Kaya.

He only hoped he was strong enough now to protect those he loved.

27

Kaya moved through the world as though trapped in a dream. Contact with the shadow left mind, spirit, and body reeling, searching for balance. She led Radyn through the maze of hallways she had once called home, the sense of familiarity clashing against the upheaval her fight had caused. Her body felt as though it moved of its own accord, pulled forward by the invisible strings of fate.

Memories of the immediate future haunted her vision. The cube's final defense had imprinted itself deeply upon her mind, and with every corner they turned, she faced a decision the cube had already shown her. Radyn no doubt questioned her cold-hearted choices, but any delay was fatal. Nightkeep's clan and Singers were after them, and any delay meant they'd be caught.

And if they were caught, they were killed, and Firestone punished by Veylan and Father.

There was no one single future, no fate that couldn't be avoided. It was all choices, thousands of choices, millions of choices, almost every one perceived as meaningless at the moment, that carved their destiny. Limited by her mind's ability to remember, she pulled them through the hallways, dodging any obstacles that stood in their way.

She threaded the narrow path that prevented Radyn from having to draw his maniblade again, for in those futures the shadow had shown her, if he drew his maniblade, they both died. His skill was a product of an aligned body and spirit, and that alignment was now shattered. For how long, she couldn't say. Perhaps forever.

Not that he wasn't still a skilled Sword. A lifetime of training and experience made him dangerous. Against the enemies he would have to face, though, it wasn't enough.

Her spirit broke for his, but they had no time to mourn. A left at an intersection delayed their return to Nightkeep's Engine but avoided a patrol of Daggers about to come around the corner of the next intersection. She hurried them through the next crossing before they were spotted by a suspicious Shield. They took the stairs three at a time to outrun a group of Swords responding to a cry for help, and eventually, they reached the level of the Engine.

Radyn's breaths came hard, though he uttered no complaint. The cut he'd suffered at her expense wasn't immediately fatal, but he wouldn't live for long without healing, and he had to be in a world of pain.

Memories of her visions faded as the echoes of the shadow's final techniques bled from her thoughts. Helpful as they'd been, she welcomed their absence. Her head pounded with every beat of her heart as her overworked mind fought to sort through future possibility and current certainty. They were close enough to the Engine now that their course was set.

She stopped at the last intersection before the hallway that led to the Engine room entrance. She squatted low and peeked around the corner. Two Swords and two Daggers stood guard, and they shuffled around as though they were waiting for orders. She slid back and quietly reported to Radyn what she'd seen. His hand went to his maniblade, then stopped, and she swore she saw it tremble.

They were fortunate they'd beaten any further reinforcements, though she shouldn't be surprised. She'd seen this before, walked through it with shadow hovering over her every move. She even knew what she was going to say to push Radyn into the last action he wanted. "Aria and your child are on the other side of those Manirah."

The trembling in his hand stopped, even as his face paled. He set his lips in a grim line and nodded, and he connected once again with the shards in his body.

The feat never failed to impress her, for the surge of strength that flowed through him would have killed anyone else, except perhaps Jyn. He absorbed the strength and let it flow like a river through his spirit. His battered soul rang a discordant note, a guitar string hammered on too many times and out of tune.

Even so, Kaya didn't think there was anyone stronger. Scars, after all, were stronger than unbroken flesh, and his heart had been scarred and scarred again. She hoped that today would turn his life onto a different path. She couldn't promise him an end to suffering, even in a better world. But she could offer him something greater.

Radyn dashed around the corner, almost upon the Swords by the time they realized the danger they were in. It was as fast as she'd ever seen him move, and the Song she heard clear as day told her he left nothing in reserve. He fought on, each cut and kill another thin scar across his heart.

The Swords fell first, and once their bodies were cooling on the floor, the Daggers lost any chance at a future. They joined their companions and Radyn let Elora's maniblade fall silent. He kept his feelings too contained, his expression no different from what it had been before he attacked, but the song of his spirit was one out of tune note after another, a string stretched close to its breaking point.

Radyn disconnected from his shards and hooked the maniblade to his hip as Kaya strode past him and opened the door to the Engine room. They stepped inside and Kaya shut the door behind them, which would give them a few extra moments once the others arrived.

She walked straight to the Engine and took his hand in hers, but she didn't reach out to touch the Engine.

Her work wasn't done. Not quite yet.

"Radyn, there's something you need to know."

He didn't respond.

"Radyn!"

Focus returned to his eyes, and he straightened. She watched as he pushed his emotions someplace deep, where they would fester until shadow sank its hooks into him, for he was too valuable for either side of the conflict to leave him alone. "Sorry, what?"

"We dealt the shadow song a terrible blow today, but we didn't kill it. Not even close."

His shoulders slumped. "I didn't think it would be so easy."

"We had the right idea, though. There is a source, closer to the equator. In the forbidden zone. I can feel it." Her tongue felt dry and heavy in her mouth, and she couldn't bring herself to say all that she should have said. "It's where we need to go next. If we defeat the source, we defeat the shadow song. Humanity would still be fighting for survival, but the nature of that conflict would change."

"No more nuddu?"

"Or banti. Maybe not even the lost clans that have

survived on the surface, because they've tied their spirits so tightly to shadow."

His expression turned dark. "We would kill that many?"

She tried to soften the blow. "Maybe. I can't say for sure. But Radyn, the shadow song, it isn't natural. It was created. It's an abomination, a disease that will gradually eat its way across this world if we don't do anything. The Makers should have stopped it long ago, but they failed. Our next best chance to stop it is now. I'm not sure if humanity will get another."

His spirit trembled at her words, balancing on the edge of despair. It sensed the deeper truths Kaya could only hint at. If it had been within her power, Kaya would have taken the burden and lifted it from his heart. It was cruel to ask him to bear more, but fairness was no more than a myth humans wished desperately was real. She could fly mountains through the sky, but she couldn't take even a sliver of his pain away.

Nor did he ask her to. It wasn't his way, and so long as shadow never took him, it would always be his way. He accepted her charge without a word of complaint. "The forbidden zone is a large area. Can you sense the origin more closely than that?"

"No. I believe it's somewhere close to the center of the continent, but beyond that, I wasn't able to tell. If I can sense it, though, so can you. It won't be able to hide from us."

"Good." Radyn gestured with his free hand. "Then you should get us out of here before Nightkeep's Singers figure out a way to stop us."

As though his words had summoned them, there was a sudden pounding on the door. They both looked to see a man wearing Nightkeep's Master of the Song robes pressing his face against the glass. The door opened, and Nightkeep's foremost Singer stepped into the Engine room with them. He said, "Please stop! We want to speak with you."

Kaya would never believe the lies. Her time with the shadow had shown her the truth. Nightkeep only wanted her dead, and they'd say anything to make that wish a reality. She only hesitated for a moment before telling Radyn, "There's something else you need to know."

"Something that can't wait?"

"I'm afraid not."

She struggled to find the right words, discarding several options.

"I know it doesn't seem like it, but everything is the way it should be. Put your trust in the Song and in life. I do so now, with no regrets."

Radyn was no fool, and he heard the lie, or at least, the half-truth. She trusted the Song, but with regret. Of course with regret. She was a creature of desire, longing for a future that was further away than ever. She wanted Orenil and the possibilities a life with him opened. She wanted to help raise Radyn's unborn child like an aunt. She wanted to explore the mysteries of life and of the Song that remained beyond her.

Suspicions and instinct running ahead of reason, Radyn tried to pull away before he argued, but she tightened the grip on his hand and reached for the Engine. Nightkeep's Master of the Song shouted again for her to stop, desperation in the notes of his voice. Her hand touched the Engine and then she and Radyn were within, spirits carried along the paths of the Song.

Nothing in her young life compared. No matter how much she learned about the Song, no matter how close she came to understanding it, she could never shake the feeling that it was outside her. She knew it wasn't true, that the Song was as much a part of her as it was every living being, but as long as she remained embodied, flesh separated her from the heart of the mystery.

Traveling through the Engines allowed her spirit to join directly with the Song, to become a part of something much larger. When she'd danced with the Engines before, there'd always been a sense of herself and a sense of the Song, two separate energies intertwined. Her efforts then had been to bring her spirit and the Song together. Now she fought to keep her sense of self. The Song invited her in, and all she had to do was surrender her body and become a part of the Song, one harmony among many.

But Radyn needed to return to Firestone. That knowledge was all that kept her flowing forward, toward the Engine at the heart of the city Radyn still thought of as home, though he hadn't lived there for years.

She slowed their transit as they reached the Engine, her certainty wavering. There had to be another way, even if she couldn't see it.

She couldn't delay long. Radyn's spirit wore hers down within the Song, a weight around her waist while she tried to swim.

It was as it should be. And not without its benefits, as she considered the Song that surrounded her. Life was nothing but a series of trades, an advantage always coming with a disadvantage. Choice was the practice of learning which advantages were worth the disadvantages.

She held his spirit close, passing on as much as she could.

Then she took the last step through the Song, and they appeared on the balcony of Firestone's Engine room. A maniblade had cut through the door, exactly as the shadow had shown her. Her transit through the Engines left her unaffected, and she caught the movement out of the corner of her eye. Veylan stood a few paces away, and her father stood behind him.

Radyn, disoriented by the travel, stumbled as she let go of his hand. He was still one of the strongest Swords in the world, though, and he saw Veylan a moment after Kaya marked him. His hand went to his maniblade, darting for the hilt like a snake lashing out at unwary prey.

At any other moment, Kaya would have bet good money on Radyn, but the disorientation of the transit proved too great to overcome. Unnaturally clumsy fingers fumbled at the hilt, missing their first grab. His hand closed on the hilt on the second attempt, but by then, Veylan was there, bringing his weapon down. He struck Radyn across the top of the head with the bottom of his hilt, and Radyn sagged.

Kaya said a silent thanks to Veylan. The senior Sword's eyes were anguished, for he was a good man who thought his only choices were poor ones.

She pressed her hand against the Engine, and her spirit soared as Veylan's maniblade came down.

She never felt the weapon that took off her head.

28

Radyn stumbled as Kaya released his hand, the world tilting around him. Details registered a moment too late. The door he'd sealed shut was open, cut from its hinges by a maniblade. They weren't alone, either. Movement to his left pulled his attention away from the door. He connected with his shards, the Song of the Engine nearly bringing him to his knees. He reached for his maniblade, fumbled, and tried again, but the shadow already stood over him. Another blur of motion, and his head exploded in lights and pain.

The blow laid him flat on the balcony, the hard Makers' steel pressing sharply against his side and back. Stars danced in his vision, but he levered himself onto his elbows. The world swam and his ears rang. Veylan's maniblade rose above and behind Kaya's head.

She looked at Radyn and smiled. Then her vision went suddenly unfocused.

Veylan's cut was nearly perfect, the skill of a man who'd trained his entire life to wield the weapon of the Manirah.

Kaya's head slipped from her shoulders. Blood spurted into the air as arteries sought to deliver blood to a brain that could no longer receive it.

Radyn reached toward Kaya, as though desire alone could reverse the flow of time. A cry was ripped from his throat, but no one paid him any mind.

He fought to reach his feet, to seek the revenge Kaya's spirit demanded, but his chest erupted in flame and darkness crowded the edges of his vision. He called upon the Song to aid him, but the strength was more than his body could handle. The darkness that had crept close swept over him, wrapping his consciousness in the sweet embrace of oblivion.

HE WOKE in a nearly featureless room. The walls had been painted a flat white, and the lanterns glowed dimly. The bed was hard beneath his back, the mattress closer in design to a used sheet than a true mattress. He stared at the blank ceiling, blinking away the tears that welled up in his eyes.

The pains in his head and side were gone, and when he probed the wound with his finger, he felt fresh skin underneath. As he lay down, he ran through a few stretches to test the area and found it as good as new.

If only all he'd suffered could be healed so easily.

He let his eyes wander around the small room. A toilet and sink in the corner. The bed he was lying on. The door was made of thick steel with a slot for food trays and various small items to pass through. There was no handle or knob on the inside.

Radyn sighed and let his head rest back on the bed. At least they'd had the decency to heal him first. Perhaps they meant for him to stay for some time. Though all the shards remained in his body, so he couldn't say what they intended. Jyn played the game with his cards held close to his chest, and Radyn couldn't be bothered to speculate. Elora's hilt was nowhere to be found, but he formed a maniblade in his hand using only his will and the shards embedded in his body without a problem, so his choices were plenty.

Of those choices, he decided to lie on his bed and stare at the ceiling. The next move wasn't his to make, and he didn't think he would be left alone for long.

Everything is the way it should be. Put your trust in the Song and in life. I do so now, with no regrets.

Radyn swallowed hard as he remembered Veylan's maniblade passing through her neck. He remembered, too, her blank look the moment before.

He hadn't imagined it.

There was a knock on the cell door. It opened a moment later, revealing Magni. He saw Radyn awake on the bed and nodded to Jyn, who followed Magni into the cell. They left the door open behind them. Magni took up a position by the door, while Jyn came in and sat on the side of the bed. Radyn twisted and rose so he was also sitting. Jyn took Elora's maniblade from a pocket and handed it to Radyn, who dipped his head in thanks.

"You look well. How do you feel?" Jyn asked.

"Physically, I'm fine."

Jyn noted Radyn's choice of words. "I'm sorry."

The Blade of Firestone hung his head, revealing a rare unguarded moment of weakness. His posture was bent, as though the weight of the past few days physically pressed against his back and spine.

If the Blade knew or guessed at the truth, he gave no sign. Radyn almost spoke, for the truth, as it often did, would ease some of his burden. Caution stilled his tongue, though. Jyn's duties spread much wider than his own, and Radyn couldn't guess what unintended consequences his disclosures would unleash upon the world.

"What happened?" Radyn asked.

"Veylan wasn't far behind you and Kaya, as you know. He saw you disappear into the Engine and just about lost his mind. He cut through the door and searched the Engine room high and low for you, convinced it was some sort of illusion. The Singer with him, who I understand was Kaya's father, eventually told Veylan that Kaya was capable of traveling between Engines. Poor Veylan was distraught, but decided it would be wise to wait. He figured that if you were to return, it would be reasonably soon, and that if you didn't, they'd begin a hunt across the continent for the two of you. I understand there was some discussion of forcing Firestone's Singers to turn Firestone toward Underhill, which was the path the Nightkeep Singer wanted to pursue, but Veylan wasn't willing."

Jyn paused. "I think you know well enough what resulted. Veylan was as merciful as his duty allowed. He could have killed you easily enough, but settled for keeping you out of the fight. He carried out his duty regarding Kaya with one clean cut. It's a small mercy, but she didn't suffer. After, Veylan and Kaya's father left Firestone to report back to Nightkeep. I had you healed."

Radyn gestured to the room. "Why the cell?"

"You were moved before they left. I figured I could at least create the illusion that you would face some sort of justice for your actions. Speaking of which, what exactly did you do while you were gone? Word hasn't reached us yet, though if I know you, I expect it will soon."

Radyn told the greater share of his story, including Kaya's belief that the shadow song had a source that could be destroyed. He omitted the more personal aspects of their final conversations, as well as his suspicions about Kaya's fate. Jyn stood when the tale finished and gestured for Radyn to follow him. The three Manirah left the cell, and Jyn led the way to Firestone's surface.

The city was as good as empty. What citizens had been settled were in different neighborhoods or hard at work, so it felt like the middle of the night, though the lanterns along the hallway were on their midday setting. Radyn blinked as they stepped into the bright sunlight of day. Jyn turned and pointed south.

The nuddu still followed them, a few miles behind the city. Radyn frowned. "If Firestone is in the air, how are they still following us?"

Once in motion, cities were much faster than nuddu.

"My orders," Jyn explained. "I hoped to lead them farther away from Underhill, and the idea seems to be working. Our speed is roughly equivalent to the nuddu's fastest, and we keep a close eye on them. So far, it's followed us without hesitation."

Radyn closed his eyes and listened for the Song. He dropped into it with unaccustomed ease and listened for the trails the nuddu was sure to leave. He sensed it as clear as day, the shadow almost as obvious to his senses as the Song. "Just out of curiosity, can you sense it?"

Jyn and Magni shared a look. "No, we can't."

Before traveling through the Engine, he wouldn't have been able to, either. Was it the work of the Song, or of Kaya?

She had described the Seer's control over the nuddu as a dark string plucked too hard. Radyn sensed the strings, but they were quiet. The nuddu was still dangerous, of course, but without a human's malicious intelligence controlling it, Radyn's heart beat easier. "I can. The Seer no longer has control over them. In this, at least, we succeeded, even if the cost was far too high."

Radyn watched the nuddu for a bit longer, then asked, "What happens next?"

"For now, we keep leading those monsters away from Underhill. Beyond that, I'm uncertain. If you invaded Nightkeep, it seems fair to believe they'll want your head. They don't have the leverage over us they did with Kaya, though truth has rarely limited their propaganda to the other cities." Jyn sighed. "Many of the city Engines are still weakening. Nightkeep is going to push everyone to choose a side, and once they have, it won't take much to start a war. I don't suppose you have any ideas for stopping one?"

"Nothing good. I would like to dive through Firestone's archives and study what maps we have of the forbidden zone. Where are they?"

"They were moved to Underhill over the course of the summer," Jyn said.

"And you're not planning on keeping me in a cell?" Radyn asked.

"We both know the only way to keep you in a cell would be to kill you, and I have no desire to lose you and Kaya. One has been hard enough."

"Then I'm going to ask Tanwen to return me to Underhill. Aria's almost due, and it's where I belong."

"Then for now we'll keep circling Underhill," Jyn said.

"You're circling?" Radyn asked.

Jyn shrugged. "Figured it was too dangerous to get too far away. These aren't the only nuddu, you'll remember. We're only trying to keep the city safe. We're circling far enough out, the nuddu doesn't seem interested in it at all. The Singers have brought the Engine back to full strength, but Firestone is still the more tempting target. Given how strong the Engine feels to my senses, I can understand why."

Normally Radyn would have bowed when he left Jyn's presence, but not today. Logically, he couldn't fault Jyn for his choices. Maybe there were none better. Still, he'd allowed Kaya to die without lifting a finger. He nodded at Jyn, then left the Blade and his guard behind.

Footsteps hurried after him, and Radyn kept walking. Magni fell into step beside him. "I, too, am sorry. I'm sure this means little to you, but I've never seen him this torn in all my years of service."

"You don't have to worry. I'm not sure that I'll ever be able to forgive him, but that doesn't mean I don't understand his position."

Magni kept pace for a few more steps, then said, "You were there for me in a moment when I really needed someone. I just wanted to let you know that if you ever need me, for anything, all you have to do is ask, and I'll come running."

That, finally, brought Radyn to a stop. He bowed to Magni. "And for that, I thank you. I'll keep it in mind. You keep him safe. I suspect the world will get more dangerous before it gets better, and we can't lose him, either."

Magni agreed with a bow and returned to his duties.

Radyn kept his composure until he reached the relative isolation of the Nest. He found Tanwen huddled into a ball that was, at least for a dragon, small. Radyn put his hand on Tanwen's neck, then shuddered as the dragon's grief mixed with his own. His lower lip trembled and he half-sat, half-collapsed beside his old friend. The shards connected them, and their sorrow was shared between them, a cup of bitter wine that seemed to have no bottom.

Radyn squeezed his eyes shut and rocked, the weight

upon his chest so great he was sure it would crush his ribs and leave him broken and shattered.

Some burdens were simply too great to bear, and he did not try. He would never see her smile again, never hear her laugh, never face her judgment for a risky decision. Nothing would fill the hole she'd left in his heart.

He leaned back and finally let his tears fall. When the well of sorrow ran dry, leaving him with nothing but emptiness, he stood.

Aria waited for him, and thanks to Kaya, he was alive. He would witness the birth of his child and not fear that a nuddu's footstep would end them all.

It wasn't enough to fill the void within, but it wasn't nothing, either. Radyn climbed slowly onto Tanwen's back, and the dragon dropped off the side of Firestone and flew gently toward Underhill.

Life went on. The Song of the Engines played on.

Radyn wanted no more part in the fight, but he had little choice. Kaya's spirit demanded revenge, and if Nightkeep wanted war, it was a war they would get. He wouldn't rest until the shadow song was destroyed for good.

THE ADVENTURES CONTINUE!

Top of the morning!

I hope that wherever you are in the world, this finds you doing well. Thanks for reading, and I hope you enjoyed the story. In an age of endless entertainment options, the choice to spend your time in these pages means the world to me.

The Silence Between the Songs was an absolute pleasure to write, and I'm excited to share more of this story over the coming year.

Before you go, I'd encourage you to sign up for my newsletter. In a world where everybody seems to be spamming people every 20 minutes to make a dime, I'm trying to do something different. I email every two to three weeks, usually on a Friday, and I do everything I can to make the newsletter something you'll look forward to reading. Free short stories that expand the worlds. Special offers. Fun conversations with fans. It would mean the world to me if you came over and took a look. You can sign up here:

https://ryankirkauthor.com/pages/newsletter-sign-up

And once again, thank you for being here. You're awesome.

Ryan

August 2025

ACKNOWLEDGMENTS

No author works alone, and I'm reminded of that every time I go through the process of releasing a new book. From the team of editors that helps clean up my words to the graphic designers who turn my scribbles into cover art, what you hold in your hands is the work of a team of dedicated professionals. To all of you, thank you.

As always, a tremendous thanks to my family. None of this would be possible without them, and all of this is for them.

And finally, a very special thanks to those readers who are part of my ARC team - picking through these books for errors and being willing to leave reviews to bring new readers in. If I miss anyone, I'm sorry - the fault is my own.

Thanks in this book, especially to:

Chuck

Terry

Neil

Terry F

Chris

and

Karen

And one final, very special thank you to all of you reading. I couldn't do this without you.

Sincerely,

Ryan

ALSO BY RYAN KIRK
FIND THEM ALL AT RYANKIRKAUTHOR.COM

Saga of the Broken Gods

Band of Broken Gods

Fall of Forgotten Gods

Rise of the Resurrected God

Last Sword in the West

Last Sword in the West

Eyes of the Hidden World

A Sword Named Vengeance

Wraith's Revenge

Frontier's End

Song of the Sagani

Legend of the Last Sword in the West

Song of the Fallen Swords

These Fallen Swords

Night of Sword and Shield

The Song of Rising Shadow

Oblivion's Gate

The Gate Beyond Oblivion

The Gates of Memory

The Gate to Redemption

Relentless

Relentless Souls

Heart of Defiance

Their Spirit Unbroken

The Nightblade Series

Nightblade

World's Edge

The Wind and the Void

Blades of the Fallen

Nightblade's Vengeance

Nightblade's Honor

Nightblade's End

Standalone Novels

Blades of Shadow

The Last Fang of God

Of Blood and Broken Dreams

The Primal Series

Primal Dawn

Primal Darkness

Primal Destiny

ABOUT THE AUTHOR

Ryan Kirk is the award-winning and internationally bestselling author of over forty fantasy novels spanning nearly a dozen worlds. He lives in Minnesota with his family, where he enjoys long, meandering walks outside even when the snow is high enough to cover his legs. When he isn't glued to his keyboard, he's usually in the woods, either on foot or on a bike.

RyanKirkAuthor.com
contact@waterstonemedia.net

 facebook.com/waterstonemedia

 x.com/waterstonebooks

 instagram.com/waterstonebooks